Max

'A perfectly poised autumnal masterpiece. Only a master of the craft of the novel could write a book of non-fiction of such quiet power and beauty.' —Robert Manne, *The Age*

'A successful combination of the life of Max Blatt and the gripping story of the author's search for him.' —Charmian Brinson, Emeritus Professor of German, Imperial College London

'A wonderful book. Miller is faithful to Max Blatt's story, to his silences and to his sadness. It is a story that needs to be heard.' —Jay Winter, Charles J. Stille Professor of History, Yale University

'With *Max*, Miller the novelist has written a wonderful work of non-fiction, as fine as the best of his novels. Always a truth-seeker, he has rendered himself vulnerable, unprotected by the liberties permitted to fiction. *Max* is perhaps his most moving book, a poignant expression of piety, true to his mentor's injunction to write with love.' —Raimond Gaita, Emeritus Professor of Moral Philosophy, King's College London, and award-winning author of *Romulus, My Father*

'A long, deeply absorbing and moving detective story . . . a celebration of the way [Max Blatt] is remembered, with all the inevitable gaps and imperfections, in the lives of those who follow him.' —*Australian Book Review*

'There is a slow, elegant circling in the storytelling, as if Miller is holding the precious shards up to the light and gently turning them to reveal their every facet . . . [*Max*] offers a deeply moving meditation on history, imagination and truth, and portrays a fascinating, visceral wrestling with facts.' —*Weekend Australian*

'A powerful, humane portrait of a man who suffered immense loss.' —*The Age*

'A moving and masterfully written testament to the power of friendship.' —*The Guardian*

'*Max* is haunted by devastating insights . . . Miller's intelligent love has created a tale for the ages.' —*Sydney Morning Herald*

'Beautifully written, engaging, deeply human . . . a book to savour and to pass among your friends.' —*Canberra Times*

The Passage of Love

'Miller's story is long, intense and vital.' —Geordie Williamson

'*The Passage of Love* is capacious, wise, and startlingly honest about human frailty and the permutations of love over time. Frankly autobiographical, it is also a work of fully achieved fiction, ripe with experience, double-voiced, peopled with unpredictable men and women, and set in Miller's landscapes that characteristically throb with life.' —Morag Fraser, 'Books of the Year', *Australian Book Review*

'Half a dozen of Miller's novels are likely to be judged among the finest of the past quarter century. They were written in the course of a career that has showcased Miller's subtlety, narrative craft, moral acuity and delight in writing about what he loves.' —*Weekend Australian*

'Conflicting demands that can throttle creativity are a big motif in this bildungsroman . . . A thoughtful autobiographical work by an award-winning Australian novelist . . . traces themes of art and commitment through Crofts' relationships with three women. Miller pulls back from the narrative several times in interludes that return to the first person of the much older man and highlight how memory has many layers. A rich addition to the growing shelf of autofiction from a seasoned storyteller.' —*Kirkus* (starred review)

'. . . delivers an enthralling fusion of fiction and memoir.' —Tom Griffiths, Books of the Year, *Australian Book Review*

'While Miller's novels are immediately accessible to the general reading public, they are manifestly works of high literary serious-ness—substantial, technically masterly and assured, intricately interconnected, and of great imaginative, intellectual and ethical weight.' —Robert Dixon in *Alex Miller: The Ruin of Time*

'It is riveting and a masterpiece in every way . . . great emotional depth . . . a magnificent achievement.' —Nicholas Birns, Professor of English at the New School in New York and author of *Contemporary Australian Literature*

'*The Passage of Love* is a novel that explicitly revisits aspects of Miller's life with the aim of shedding light on subjects beyond its biographical orbit . . . a slow-burning catalogue of marital breakdown enlivened only by Miller's trademark prose, limpid and grave and stately in progression, each sentence fragment tongue-and-grooved with the next.' —*Australian Book Review*

'An intimate book . . . Miller has a gift for examining the domestic and exploring private lives.' —*Good Reading*

'*The Passage of Love* offers an insight into a great writer's journey . . . Miller maintains a tangible sense of place throughout, in particular, the landscape of isolated country NSW. This novel is a must for fans of Miller.' —*Books+Publishing*

'There is something elegiac about *The Passage of Love*, in its detailing of a vanished 1950s Melbourne, in the passion and urgency of its fierce protagonist . . . Miller's writing has the muscularity of decades-earned craft, spare and unsentimental, probing the sinews of marriage, delineating the arc of love affairs, of struggle and disappointment.' —*Irish Times*

'Miles Franklin award-winner Miller has crafted a novel that's individual in its essence with originality and sensitivity.' —*PS News*

'*The Passage of Love* is a gift. It tells us about living with an undeniable creative force and the consequences of being utterly transparent in one's desires. It is an observation, a sharing of knowledge and a transcript of a life lived with yearning . . . Extraordinary.' —*Readings*

'The most candid, sharing, generous book I've read in a long, long time.' —ABC Radio

'A great read with profound insights into the nature of love and creativity.' —*Australian Financial Review*

'An exquisitely personal life story told in a fictional style . . . Miller draws on memories, dreams, stories, love and death to create a moving and raw fictional novel that is the closest to an autobiography likely to be read from him. In a rich blend of thoughtful and beautifully observed writing, the lives of a husband and wife are laid bare in their passionate struggle to engage with their individual creativity.' —*Highlife*

The Simplest Words

'Most collections of this kind are interesting and useful reminders of the value of a writer of considerable literary standing. *The Simplest Words* is more powerful than that, because of Miller's intense engagement with his subjects, and because Stephanie Miller has chosen pieces that speak to one another, accounting, in a way, for one of our most original, engagingly vehement and expansive writers.' —Brenda Walker, *Australian Book Review*

'This is a rich, generous compilation that enticingly refracts our perceptions of one of Australia's finest novelists.' —Peter Pierce, *The Age*

'[Miller's] writing has a luminous quality that sings off the page and whether he is writing on family, friendship, memory or just life, he engages with the reader, involving them in his orbit.' —Helen Caples and Martin Stevenson, *The Examiner*

Coal Creek

'Miller's voice is never more pure or lovely than when he channels it through an instrument as artless as Bobby . . . The intelligence of the author haunts the novel, like an atmosphere.' —Geordie Williamson, *The Monthly*

'. . . a master of visceral description.' —*Weekend Australian*

'Because of this subdued mode of storytelling, the tension mounts gradually and when tragedy strikes it is truly, hideously, mesmerising . . . an evocative and moving novel of the Australian bush.' —*Books+Publishing*

'*Coal Creek* is a story of friendship, love, loyalty and the consequences of mistrust set against Miller's exquisite depictions of the country of the Queensland highlands.' —*Books and Arts Daily*

Autumn Laing

'Such riches. All of Alex Miller's wisdom and experience—of art, of women and what drives them, of writing, of men and their ambitions—and every mirage and undulation of the Australian landscape are here, transmuted into rare and radiant fiction. An indispensable novel.' —*Australian Book Review*

'. . . in many respects Miller's best yet . . . a penetrating and moving examination of long-dead dreams and the ravages of growing old.' —*Times Literary Supplement*

'A beautiful book.' —*Irish Times*

'Miller's prose is so simply wrought it almost disguises its sophistication . . .
The result transforms one woman's dying words into pure and living
art.' —*Weekend Australian*

'. . . a magisterial work . . . a compulsively readable tale.'
—*The Advertiser*

'Miller has invested this story of art and passion with his own
touch of genius and it is, without question, a triumph of a novel.'
—*Canberra Times*

'Miller engages so fully with his female characters that divisions
between the sexes seem to melt away and all stand culpable, vulnerable, human on equal ground. Miller is also adept at taking abstract
concepts—about art or society—and securing them in the convincing
form of his complex, unpredictable characters and their vivid interior
monologues.' —*The Monthly*

'Few writers have Miller's ability to create tension of this depth out
of old timbers such as guilt, jealousy, selfishness, betrayal, passion
and vision. *Autumn Laing* is more than just beautifully crafted. It is
inhabited by characters whose reality challenges our own.' —*The Age*

'Miller's long honing of the craft of his fiction has never been seen to
better advantage than in *Autumn Laing*.' —*Sydney Morning Herald*

'Nowhere in Miller's work has the drama of character been so well
synthesised with the drama of ideas. Nowhere else have his characters
drunk ideas like wine and exhaled them like cigarette smoke, a philosophical questing indistinguishable from defiant bohemian excess.'
—*Weekend Australian*

Lovesong

'With *Lovesong*, one of our finest novelists has written perhaps his finest book . . . *Lovesong* explores, with compassionate attentiveness, the essential solitariness of people. Miller's prose is plain, lucid, yet full of plangent resonance.' —*The Age*

'*Lovesong* is a ravishing, psychologically compelling work from one of our best.' —*Courier-Mail*

'Miller's brilliant, moving novel captures exactly that sense of a storybuilt life—wonderful and terrifying in equal measure, stirring and abysmal, a world in which both heaven and earth remain present, yet stubbornly out of reach.' —*Sunday Age*

'*Lovesong* is another triumph: lyrical, soothing and compelling. Miller enriches human fragility with literary beauty . . .' —*Newcastle Herald*

'Alex Miller's novel *Lovesong* is a limpid and elegant study of the psychology of love and intimacy. The characterisation is captivating and the framing metafictional narrative skilfully constructed.' —*Australian Book Review*

'The intertwining stories are told with gentleness, some humour, some tragedy and much sweetness. Miller is that rare writer who engages the intellect and the emotions simultaneously, with a creeping effect.' —*Bookseller & Publisher*

'With exceptional skill, Miller records the ebb and flow of emotion . . . *Lovesong* is a poignant tale of infidelity; but it is more than that. It is a manifesto for the novel, a tribute to the human rite of fiction with the novelist officiating.' —*Australian Literary Review*

Landscape of Farewell

'The latest novel by the Australian master, so admired by other writers, and a work of subtle genius.' —Sebastian Barry

'*Landscape of Farewell* is a triumph.' —Hilary McPhee

'Alex Miller is a wonderful writer, one that Australia has been keeping secret from the rest of us for too long.' —John Banville

'As readers of his previous novels—*The Ancestor Game, Prochownik's Dream, Journey to the Stone Country*—will know, Miller is keenly interested in inner lives. *Landscape of Farewell* continues his own quest, and in doing so, speaks to his reader at the deepest of levels. He juggles philosophical balls adroitly in prose pitched to an emotional perfection. Every action, every comma, is loaded with meaning. As one expects from the best fiction, the novel transforms the reader's own inner life. Twice winner of the Miles Franklin Award, it is only a matter of time before Miller wins a Nobel. No Australian has written at this pitch since Patrick White. Indeed, some critics are comparing him with Joseph Conrad.' —*Daily News*, New Zealand

'*Landscape of Farewell* has a rare level of wisdom and profundity. Few writers since Joseph Conrad have had so fine an appreciation of the equivocations of the individual conscience and their relationship to the long processes of history . . . [It is] a very human story, passionately told.' —*Australian Book Review*

Prochownik's Dream

'Assured and intense ... truly gripping ... This is a thoroughly engrossing piece of writing about the process of making art, a revelatory transformation in fact.' —*Bookseller & Publisher*

'With this searing, honest and exhilarating study of the inner life of an artist, Alex Miller has created another masterpiece.' —*Good Reading*

Journey to the Stone Country

'The most impressive and satisfying novel of recent years. It gave me all the kinds of pleasure a reader can hope for.' —Tim Winton

'A terrific tale of love and redemption that captivates from the first line.' —Nicholas Shakespeare, author of *The Dancer Upstairs*

Conditions of Faith

'This is an amazing book. The reader can't help but offer up a prayerful thank you: Thank you, God, that human beings still have the audacity to write like this.' —*Washington Post*

'I think we shall see few finer or richer novels this year . . . a singular achievement.' —Andrew Riemer, *Australian Book Review*

The Ancestor Game

'A wonderful novel of stunning intricacy and great beauty.' —Michael Ondaatje

'For pure delight, abandon the maze, and read for sensual pleasure. This is a gift of floors of lacquered Baltic pine, pearwood shelves and tea boxes. There is the perfume of the camphor laurel trees, coats made of the pelts of 18 grey foxes, and Victoria Tang's horse. Smell the porridge and sour pickles, cross the cold wet slate court-yard flagstones. Remember chrysanthemums the deep rust color of an old fox's scalp.' —Sara Sanderson, *Indianapolis News*

'A major new novel of grand design and rich texture, a vast canvas of time and space, its gaze outward yet its vision intimate and intel-lectually abundant.' —*The Age*

'A dense, complex work that addresses the issues of cultural displace-ment, colonialism and the individual's imaginative link to earlier generations . . . Extraordinary fictional portraits of China and Australia.' —*New York Times Book Review*

'One of the most engrossing books I've read in a long time.' —Robert Dessaix

'Takes the historical novel to new frontiers. It is fabulous in every sense of the word.' —Commonwealth Writers Prize judges

The Sitters

'Like Patrick White, Miller uses the painter to portray the ambivalence of art and the artist. In *The Sitters* is the brooding genius of light. Its presence is made manifest in Miller's supple, painterly prose which layers words into textured moments.' —Simon Hughes, *Sunday Age*

The Tivington Nott

'*The Tivington Nott* abounds in symbols to stir the subconscious. It is a rich study of place, both elegant and urgent. An extraordinarily gripping novel.' —*Melbourne Times*

Also by Alex Miller

Max

The Passage of Love

The Simplest Words

Coal Creek

Autumn Laing

Lovesong

Landscape of Farewell

Prochownik's Dream

Journey to the Stone Country

Conditions of Faith

The Sitters

The Ancestor Game

The Tivington Nott

Watching the Climbers on the Mountain

A
BRIEF
AFFAIR

ALEX MILLER

A BRIEF AFFAIR

ALLEN&UNWIN
SYDNEY • MELBOURNE • AUCKLAND • LONDON

First published in 2022

Allen & Unwin
Cammeraygal Country
83 Alexander Street
Crows Nest NSW 2065
Australia
Phone: (61 2) 8425 0100
Email: info@allenandunwin.com
Web: www.allenandunwin.com

Allen & Unwin acknowledges the Traditional Owners of the Country on which we live and work. We pay our respects to all Aboriginal and Torres Strait Islander Elders, past and present.

A catalogue record for this book is available from the National Library of Australia

ISBN 978 1 76106 657 3

Internal design by Bookhouse, Sydney
Set in 13/20 pt Granjon by Bookhouse, Sydney
Printed and bound in Australia by Griffin Press

10 9 8 7 6 5 4 3 2 1

for Stephanie

&

for my mother and her old people, the Egans of Ballyragget

ONE

B efore she had a shower, and still in her dressing-gown, Fran sat on the edge of the bed and wrote in her diary. It was Wednesday. The middle of her first week back already. Since China she hadn't been able to find her old enthusiasm for the job. And anyway, the new campus was haunted. She had the unsettling feeling of being unwelcome there. She didn't believe in the paranormal and ghosts or anything like that, of course, but at the same time the place was creepy. She wrote: *The sense of unease or even horror in a place where terrible things have happened is familiar to me.* She had been meaning to make this note ever since she began working at the Sunbury campus, but for some reason she had never quite got around to doing it. It had nagged at her. Now it was done. It was on paper.

She read over what she'd written. It would do. Her feeling was on the record. But her question remained: What is that residue of unease which is left behind like a stain on old wallpaper long after the deed? What does it speak of to us? What is it we *know* in our skin when we feel that chill? Other people felt it too. Not everyone. Not Carlos Skänder, the Dean of Studies. Carlos claimed to feel nothing. Which was probably the truth. But some of her colleagues did, enough of them to reassure Fran that it wasn't just her own fancy. She closed her diary and slipped it into her laptop case, then she stood up from the bed, took off her dressing-gown and looked at herself in the wardrobe mirror. She ran her hands over her belly and lightly touched the moon-shaped scar on the inside of her left thigh. Until China, she had always thought of the scar as her wound. She and her best friend Penny, when they were ten, clambering around on the roof of the abandoned house next door, and the awful scream that came out of her as the roof collapsed under them. When her mother arrived, she gave her attention and sympathy to Penny, who'd received only a small cut to her scalp, and told Fran to get up and stop making such a fuss. Watching her mother attending to Penny that day, the pieces of the puzzle came together for Fran and she understood in a flash that her mother was not withholding her love but was unable to love her. Simply that. And she made what seemed to her then to be the first real decision of her life: she would cease begging for her mother's love and would rely on herself. The wound, after all, was for life.

Margie was singing in the kitchen. Fran took a shower, then got dressed. She had dreamed she gave birth to a male child. It was suddenly there. It lay asleep on her bed. When she looked at it, its eyes opened and it began to assess her, coldly. Her secret life was open to it. She had no love for it. Seeing it there had made her nervous.

* * *

Dressed for the day ahead, a smart-looking woman of forty-two, her satchel on her shoulder, her laptop case in her left hand, Dr Frances Egan came out the back door and headed for her car. The landscape of field and farm was at peace. The rusted tin roof of the old stone cottage down the hill glistening with frost, a soft white mist lying along the creek flats below the house, the sound of the creek in the perfection of morning stillness. Tom stood in the doorway behind her, holding the flywire door open, watching her leave. He watched her walking away from him along the gravel drive towards the old stable, where her yellow Renault was parked, the touch of her lips still cool on his cheek. Little Tommy came and stood beside his father and called, 'Bye, Mum!' At the boy's anxious cry, she turned and waved and called back to him, a catch in her voice, 'Bye, darling!'

They stood, watching her leave, the man and the boy, and when she stepped on a loose stone and appeared to stumble, they both flinched and would have run to her aid, but she recovered and went on, her free hand pointing down at the offending stone. Then she was gone, but they still stood, man and boy, in the cold air, as if a question remained with them, a pale dust in the stillness of the morning where she had been. They might have been watching the flight of galahs now that swerved across the lower paddock to settle and feed on the roots of the onion grass.

* * *

She parked at the railway station and found a seat on the train. She didn't open her laptop but sat looking out the window, watching the countryside sliding by. Grey clouds were banking up from the south and thickening the light. It was probably going to rain later after all, despite the confident forecast of fine weather from the bureau. Seeing the beauty of the glossy red cattle and the scatter of white sheep grazing on the vivid green winter grass with its glistening patches of frost, Fran was invaded by a familiar wave of sadness. A sob gathered in her throat and she closed her eyes. The shriek of the train's warning made her open her eyes again. A line of shining cars waited at the level crossing as the train thundered past, its whistle howling—the battle cry of a triumphant enemy who would scatter them all to hell.

She closed her eyes again. In the warm compartment of the speeding train it was a reassurance and a terror to think of him. She did not resist the memory. She could not resist it. It came, vivid and unbidden, into her head.

A t the hotel in Hefei the man behind the check-in desk said
to her, haughty in his delivery, 'We are a star hotel. We
don't take credit cards.' She had thought this amusing. It was
the strangeness of China. When she went down later, the
others—the ambassador's wife with her lady companion, two
colleagues from home and some people she did not know—were
gathered in the foyer, a knot of Westerners, her own people,
waiting for the minibus that was to take them to the university.
The ambassador's wife said to her, 'Is this your first visit to
China, Frances?' Fran was looking out through the glass doors,
along the driveway to where a large open square was busy with
pedestrians and bicycle and truck traffic. It was raining gently,

everything shining, as if the scene received a soft grey lacquer of approval. 'China,' she murmured. She was excited. Nervous and excited, and intensely curious to see and hear and smell everything, to take China into her and have something real from it to take back with her. Now that she was actually in China, she realised the few words of Mandarin she had managed to learn were like a random handful of pebbles in her brain, small and round and distinct, not connected as words in language are connected, like words in French and in her mother tongue. She turned to the ambassador's wife, whose name she had failed to remember. 'I think I'll catch a bus,' she said.

The ambassador's wife laughed. It was the scornful, dismissive laugh of the old hand for the newcomer. 'Oh, yes. And you'll get lost.' She spoke loudly, so everyone would hear her and know she was the biggest woman in the group, the wife of the ambassador. She had announced the evening before, as if it were her pride, 'I don't speak Chinese.' It wasn't very diplomatic of her. And, she had added, 'I'm an Australian.' It was the pride of the white Australian caste of the native born speaking. That familiar sense of spurious entitlement bestowed by the accident of birth. 'Yes, dear. You will get lost.'

'I'll risk that,' Fran said. She smiled at the ambassador's wife. You are so fucking condescending, she thought and broadened her smile. She was determined not to let herself be put down by people who claimed to be of a higher status. An ambassador's wife, she thought, is not, after all, an ambassador. 'I don't mind getting lost.' The ambassador's wife, she noticed, had watery eyes, poor thing, and her legs were stumpy. Too bad for her.

Fran stood by the side of the road watching as the yellow minibus drove away from the hotel, the faces of her party pale ovals at the windows, insulated from being really in China. She thought them timid and lacking in curiosity. You are not *in* China. You are in a minibus looking out at China. She felt contempt for them and laughed.

* * *

Alone in the busy square, Fran stood and watched in awe a truck laden to an impossible height with crates of eggs. As it turned around the square, its reflection in the wet surface of the black road. Slowly the great load began to heel over like a sailing boat hit by a squall, the near-side wheels of the truck lifting from the road in an unstoppable dream, the anguish on the face of the driver behind the windscreen. When the load hit the road a great flood of egg yolks flowed outwards across the steaming surface of the tar. Fran stood transfixed by the sight of dozens of people who appeared with buckets and saucepans and began scooping up the flood of egg. The truck driver scrambled out of his cabin like a man coming up out of a manhole. He jumped to the ground and shouted at her, waving his fist. She feared he wished to seek his revenge on the

Western woman observing his shame. She turned and walked quickly away, not daring to look back in case he was coming after her, the heat of his anger driving him to an extreme. Her heart was beating quickly.

Now deeply into the square, she wandered among the makeshift alleyways of the food market. Every part of slaughtered beasts was for sale, string bags of sheep's eyeballs and buckets of pink bird entrails. The light rain dripping from the canvas awnings. The people manning their booths were strangely idle, smoking cigarettes and talking and looking about. No one was spruiking their wares. They seemed to her not eager for customers but mildly curious about the outcome of the day. Everyone she saw was Chinese. They looked at her but no one smiled. The rain began to come down more heavily, water dripping from the awnings of the booths onto the black cobbles. The narrow lanes between the booths sloped gently towards the centre, where they formed a natural drain.

Fran was standing under the shelter of an awning when she saw a man lying face down in the drain on the narrow roadway. He was working himself along the lane with his elbows and pushing a tin ahead of him with his chin. The man's eyes were fixed on her. Fran was so shocked by this sight that she didn't think to put money in the tin but just watched the agonising progress of the beggar until he had gone past her. The empty trouser legs of his suit trailed along the drain behind him, black and soaked. She felt a hand on her arm and, at the same moment, a woman's voice close to her said, 'Do you speak English?' The woman was Chinese and about Fran's age. She smiled and said, 'Come, I have something that has been waiting for you.'

Fran let herself be led by the woman to a nearby stall filled with antiques and curios. There was scarcely space enough inside for the two of them. The woman picked up a green glazed parrot and offered it to Fran. Fran took the parrot in her hand and looked at it. It was remarkably light. The likeness of the piece to a real parrot was not detailed but was more the general idea of a parrot, the form and shape of a bird with its wings folded along its body, its beak with the unmistakable hook of a parrot's. Fran decided to buy it.

'How much do you want for it?'

The woman smiled. 'It is old. Hundreds of years old. But you can't just buy it on its own. The pair must stay together.' She handed Fran another green parrot of exactly the same kind as the one already in her hand.

Fran said, 'I'll just buy one, thank you. One green parrot will be enough for me.'

The woman smiled and pressed the second parrot on her. 'In China,' she said, 'it is bad luck to have just one of a pair. Pairs should never be separated or bad luck will follow you wherever you go afterwards.'

Fran set the second parrot back on the trestle beside her. 'In Australia, we believe that it is bad luck to ever buy things in pairs. In Australia you will never see a pair of anything.' She looked steadily into the eyes of the woman. 'My family and all my friends would begin to avoid me if I returned from China with a pair of green parrots.' Fran saw that the woman was hesitating so she pressed her advantage. 'I once knew a man who bought a pair of owls. Not long after this he developed lung cancer and died.'

The woman looked quite worried by this story. 'That is true?'

'Oh yes.' Fran crossed her heart and held the woman's gaze. 'It is the truth. How much is just one green parrot?'

The woman stared at the parrot in Fran's hand. 'It is an antique. You cannot buy such a rare parrot for less than one thousand seven hundred yuan.'

Fran looked at the parrot again. She turned it over and looked at the bottom, then she looked steadily into the woman's eyes again. There was, she thought, the faintest flicker of amusement in the woman's expression. 'Well then,' Fran said, 'I'll give you fifty yuan for it.'

The woman said, 'All right. Do you want me to wrap it up for you?'

They both laughed and the woman put her hand on Fran's arm. 'You are the first Australian I have ever met. I shan't forget that Australians never come in pairs.' She wrapped the parrot in newspaper and tied it with a piece of twine and handed it to Fran, and Fran handed her a fifty-yuan note.

Before leaving the woman and her antique stall, Fran showed her the conference invitation, on which the address of the university was written in Chinese underneath the English, and asked her where she could catch a bus. The woman took Fran by the arm and led her out into the square. She pointed to a bus stop. 'The number one six nine.'

After crossing the road, Fran turned. The woman was standing watching her. She waved and Fran waved back, then continued on towards the bus stop. She was surprised now to realise how untouched she had been by the man dragging himself along by his elbows. She might have dreamed the Hefei market except that the green parrot in her bag was real. The crowd had dispersed, but the capsized egg truck still lay on its side, an obstacle diverting the flow of traffic.

* * *

The bus was half empty. No one looked at her when she got on. She was alone in the vastness of China's hinterland, a green parrot that was probably worth no more than five yuan in her bag. She sat by a window and looked out. 'Yes,' she murmured aloud, 'it's my first visit to China. And I've just been done by an expert.'

She loved sitting on the bus, anonymous. She felt free from the cares of real life. The bus going from stop to stop, picking passengers up and setting others down. She was a part of it, just as if she had magically become a Chinese woman alone on a bus. Her responsible self, her old self, only a little anxious that she would not know when to get off and would miss the university stop. In a way the ambassador's wife might yet be right; it didn't matter to Fran just then if she really did get lost. For days. Forever. Perhaps she would find a new life and never return to Tom and the kids and the farm. Would the world then come to an end for her, after all? Would it? What a question! One world would end and another begin.

The bus was filling up. A man got on and sat in the vacant seat beside her. She felt his weight, sitting there, not fidgeting, his presence still, silent and heavy. She thought, A man of substance. Was he Chinese? The faint smell of the rain on his woollen overcoat. He was wearing a smart business suit under his coat and carried an umbrella and a briefcase. The only such person on the bus. She wanted to turn and look at him. He did not look at her. Wasn't he curious? She was the only non-Chinese woman on the bus. No one had looked at her. Did they not have any curiosity? Or were they too polite? She resisted looking at him and continued looking out the window, aware of being like *them*, aware of being not herself. If only she could muster those little pebbles of sound and make something of them, she might speak to this man. He was obviously educated and would not mind being spoken to by a foreigner.

At the next stop she turned and she did look at him, becoming at once Western again. He gazed straight ahead. His features in profile were flat, powerful, his manner interior, and beautiful. She thought of a Mongol warrior. A horseman of the steppe. Exotically seductive. The thrill in her belly was delicious, secret, lovely. She hadn't had that feeling for years. She was a young girl again. She had thought it was over. The bus moved on and, slowly, he turned his head and looked at her. They observed each other in silence. The intensity of it was making her breathless. Then he said, 'Where do you come from?'

Her breath failed her altogether and she cleared her throat. 'I'm an Australian.'

'I know you are an Australian,' he said gravely, as if her origins were known to him. 'Where, in Australia, do you come from?'

His English was soft and rounded and filled with quiet self-assurance, an assertion of inner confidence. His gaze steady.

'From Victoria.'

'Where in Victoria?'

She breathed, feeling the warm blood rising to her cheeks. 'A small town near Bendigo. It's in the country.'

'What small town?'

She laughed. He did not smile.

'We have a farm,' she said. 'Our closest town is called Newstead.'

'And do you go to the Newstead pub for lunch sometimes?'

'You can't possibly know the Newstead pub!' she cried, and laughed aloud.

The woman sitting across the aisle looked at her with a sharp, quick turn of her head. Or did she look at him?

Now he smiled. The smile in his eyes bewitched her.

The horseman of the steppe looked into her eyes and smiled at her. The pulse of erotic pleasure at that intimate place in her lower abdomen, a pulse she had known as a girl in school—it was still alive! She allowed herself to say into the silence of her secrecy, I want to make love with this man. 'Who are you?' she asked. But, of course, she already knew he must be an academic on his way to attend the international management conference she was going to herself. Was she not the dean's emissary, out there in the remoteness of it, to sell their executive residential short courses? An expensive enterprise. A woman of responsibility.

His smile broadened. He was reading her secret thoughts. For an infinite moment it was as if he might not answer her but might enjoy her disbelief, the inspiration of her lust, his attention intimate and observant. Then he spoke again and the bus jolted over a pothole in the road, tossing them about.

He said, 'I spent six months as a visiting professorial fellow at the university of La Trobe in Bendigo. The couple I lived with took me to the Newstead pub for lunch several times. There is a photograph of me with them on the wall behind the bar. You may know them—Professor Michael Rowland and his wife Diedre Macklen?'

'Of course. Yes, I know Michael well.'

'When you get home, you can go to the Newstead pub and have a look. You must know that the Newstead pub is famous for the lunch it provides to travellers.'

She did know. They had gone there as a family the day she and Tom made their successful offer on the farm. The perfect family having an outing; little Tommy and Margie, she and Tom. Her husband, her family. The clarity of their perfection evident to everyone who saw them. Lunch under a sun umbrella in the side garden of the pub. City people. Their laughter and the innocence of their happiness, their freedom and delight at having found the ideal little farm in the country, where the air did not smell of exhausts, her dream and Tom's. Had this man been among those who had observed them that day? An impossible coincidence, surely. The kind of thing that only happens in real life.

'And then you sat next to me,' she said.

'It was the only vacant seat left on the bus. Didn't fate arrange it for us?'

For us! They both laughed, not loudly, but privately now, sharing their secret. It was the moment their bond was sealed. He had felt it too. She was afraid now.

* * *

That night in the hotel in Hefei the noble Mongolian horseman came to her bed and she had no fear of him. They made love without words. Naked between the sheets together, she fell with him from the innocent sky and they became one. She heard him moan and knew it was herself who cried out in the ecstasy of her rapture. They were lost in each other in a place where there was no right or wrong. She was made for this moment. There was no choice. He was right. Now she too believed this to be their fate.

The train horn shrieked again and Fran opened her eyes. Her heart was pounding. Had she made a sound? She looked around quickly. They were all on their phones.

No one in this world can ever be truly exotic anymore. We are all familiars. Anything is possible. Everything is possible. When she thought of what she had done, her joy of it made her breathless and her terror of discovery was great. One day, in a moment when she had forgotten to fear it, a casual word would be spoken in Tom's presence and he would look at her and know the answer to his uncertainty and see that she had betrayed him with the Chinese man in the photograph on the wall behind the bar in the Newstead pub, the handsome stranger who stood with Professor Michael Rowland and his wife Diedre Macklen. Tom's brain would put two and two together for him. He wouldn't have to think about it. He would see the way she cast a furtive glance towards that photo and it would be clear to him in a flash, as if a shotgun was fired close to his head. His perfect trust shattered. His dream blown apart. Was that to be her story? Their story?

Thinking of her Mongolian warrior now, the train rushing through the cold landscape of the morning towards Sunbury, the perfection of her lust that night drew her back to her lover's naked body pressed against her own, the hard cool strength of the man in her arms. She could have no regrets. She closed her eyes and let herself think of them both and was swept along in the powerful sweetness of it, the terror and the bliss, a moment out of ordinary time. A gift. Their cries had been the one cry. And afterwards, unable to speak of it, they had witnessed the perfection of it in the other's gaze. He and she. She gave a little gasp. 'It is mine!' she murmured, helpless, covetous. 'It is *mine*!' There was a fierceness in her possession of it that shocked her. And before he left her in the greyness of that morning, they made love again, knowing they must seal their bond against the realities of the world that was to destroy them.

She knew the story. Everyone knew it. It was the oldest story.

As the train pulled into Sunbury station and came to a halt, she knew herself to be alone and lost. A different person. The commuters around her rising from their seats and hurrying to leave the compartment. She stood up and followed them. Familiar Sunbury station was stranger to her in the moment of stepping from the train than that hotel room in Hefei could ever be.

* * *

The air was colder than she had expected. Behind her the train gave a little shriek and moved off, continuing its journey towards the centre of Melbourne. By the time she reached the exit the platform was deserted. A wind straight from the Antarctic snatched at her. She grimaced and tugged her winter coat close around her and turned up her collar. Facing the day, the cold wind on her cheeks, Fran's features coarsened and she lost the benevolence of her beauty. It was a day her Irish mother would have described as raw. After Fran's father died, Fran asked her mother why she was returning to Ireland. Her mother said, I miss the northern twilight. Fran told her, You're being selfish. You're depriving the kids of a grandmother. Her mother went anyway. You can bring them over to see me.

Fran decided her body had turned against her. She knew in that moment she was no longer beautiful. The suburban outskirts of the city falling away behind the railway station, roof after roof cascading down the hill and spreading out into the valley, a grey unstoppable thing smothering the open country.

She turned away from the sprawl of houses and began the walk up Jacksons Hill. She had never seen her mother's old home. Kilkenny was just a romantic word for her.

Passing the last of the new housing development, the desolate smell of fresh concrete and timber in the chilly air, her ankle began to ache where she had rolled it that morning on a loose stone. Ahead of her on the summit of Jacksons Hill the vast Victorian institution, its heavy stone and red-brick wings commanding the boundaries of its parkland, a replica of a grand English nineteenth-century institution for the promotion of public order, the old lunatic asylum, the dark Scots pines resisting the wind, standing blackly against the sky before the towers and turrets, ragged and tormented by the years, dead limbs torn from their trunks still lying at the base of them, the last things to be dealt with. Built there to be seen, it was, that pile of stone and brick, designed to intimidate. Now her university's newest campus. The home of her School of Management. She paused and stood, gathering her resolve. She took her handkerchief from her bag and blew her nose. The chill had made it run. She blew it again, to be sure. Then went on.

Why did she feel no guilt for it? Why was she without regret? She refused to deny him. They had *belonged* to each other that night in Hefei, hadn't they? The two of them naked in each other's arms.

He had touched the old scar on the inside of her left thigh and made it precious with his lips. 'Your moon scar,' he said. 'Our poets sing of the moon when they wish to speak of love.' And he looked at her and smiled. 'Whenever I step outside to stand and look up at the moon, I shall think of you and I will remember this night of ours.' Since then, she could not touch her scar without feeling the pulse of him inside her. The purity of the thrill. It wasn't an affair, that sordid word. She was not a woman who had betrayed her husband with another man. She would refuse to name it that. It was simple and it was pure, unsullied and unknown, a mystery to such things as moral choice. Its source a place beyond the reach of social artifice and hostility. No one would ever understand it except the two of them. No one but they would ever *know* it. She felt no remorse. She knew in her heart she had done nothing wrong but had done something beautiful and real. With him she had touched the ideal, just for a moment, for one short everlasting night of her life. At the thought of him a gust of happiness swept over her. As she walked up the hill she smiled. And she, Dr Frances Egan, was beautiful again. 'Look at the moon,' she said aloud.

Nothing lasts, of course, she knew that, least of all moods. But this gust of happiness was surely a sign that she had regained her belief. Wasn't it?

Everything asserts its opposite.

Lying together in the purity of their nakedness, she had known her life that night to be a mystical journey of recognition, an existence without questions and without answers, but her own in a simple way that nothing else was ever simply her own—not Tom, not the children, not the farm and definitely not her job. None of it was just hers. Words could not speak of this other thing. A painting by a great artist had surely captured it, or a beautiful piece of music that reaches wordlessly into the soul and touches the source of hope in us. The sacred music at the point of her own beginning. That sacred music. She knew what she meant. She *felt* beautiful. It was all that mattered just then, so long as the gust of happiness played lightly within her mind; her beauty was all that mattered to her, the sun blessing her innocence. Beautiful and happy, for the moment she rose above her doubts. The girl she had once been had survived within her. That was it. The perfect world of her dreams was still real. It was not lost, it was not beyond reach after all. Happiness made it so. Happiness sustained the dream. Surely that is what happiness is? What are we without the dream but slaves to the treadmill of our days? Without the dream, our hopes become disillusion. It was all clear as that to her.

* * *

After China, Dr Frances Egan was no longer solitary. Within her inner world, that is, where the sacred had its being for her, that place where she was cherished. It was there that her Mongolian warrior stood with her now. Dreamers, the two of them, alone against a ruptured world.

The male child of her dream knew all. In the presence of that spectral infant the gust of happiness faltered and died in her, like an uncertain breeze, and the clouds drew together above her once again, as they will on such a day. The newborn's chilling regard of her inner world. What hidden impulse was it within her that had given her fear such a form as that? I am watching, the child's eyes said. *I know.* The dream of the knowing male child was a threat. Was it a warning? And she ignoring it, as wilful people will ignore the signs that are telling them what they don't want to hear. Your ears are closed to sense, her mother told her. It's no good me telling you anything.

It was her blissful transgression that spawned it. The thousands of broken eggs reappeared in her dreams. The truck driver's rage transformed the threat. It was real. The child a portent of her own doom. There was nothing she could do. Since China, Fran's life was more complicated and more real than it had ever been. She had been shocked out of the old groove she had worn for herself. She had taken that step with him out into a wider place. Consequences were beyond her. She found herself waiting in expectation of the next unfolding, her nerves on edge, her mind alert for the sign that would announce it. There were moments when she longed to be the person she had been before China. She resented and feared these moments. Her moods thrashed wildly like the dark branches of the broken pines in the Antarctic wind. To be simply at peace once again; wife, mother, professional woman. Why had that not been enough for her? There was no undoing what she had done. It lived within her, its consequences would be fulfilled, it had its own being. The understanding matured in her slowly. But by the time she reached the university grounds that morning Fran had begun to see that she had left her known world behind that night in Hefei and had become a mystery to herself. The knowledge frightened her. Her instinct was to deny it. Wife, mother, professional woman. But that was not her, was it? The safe cage she had known as her familiar world. The label. How was she to hold it together now? How continue to pretend?

* * *

As Fran approached the building she hesitated, standing still a moment and looking at the great main door of the institution, as if she expected it to open. She saw that the card left by the security company was still in the door at the top of the steps, a white triangle sticking out at head height. How was she to switch her thoughts from the world of Hefei to the routine of this place? The prospect of the day ahead lay on her mind, cold and grey and impossible. She went up the steps. Happiness, that ephemeral, fleeting, winged insect in its brief and glittering flight, had touched her for a lovely moment. Surely it would return and touch her again? The door of her daily existence had not yet been nailed shut. She was still young. She could still call on her courage, couldn't she? She would have liked to sit and weep in a quiet place of her own. She fished her keys out of her bag and unlocked the door, then she got out her handkerchief and blew her nose. Just to be sure.

The sound of the heavy outer door crashing to behind her echoed through the void of the building. There was a faintly familiar smell of something chill and undisturbed in the air of the wide foyer. From where did she remember this smell? A residue of something from the past that refused to leave the fabric of this place, the ghosts of the once-upon-a-time lunatics refusing to be forgotten. There was no one about. She crossed the foyer and climbed the broad stone stairs to the upper floor. Her runners made a faint squeaky sound in the empty building. In the beginning, when she had worn heels to work, thinking herself then a kind of goddess, emboldened by her sense of her own success, her heels had struck the desolate silence of the old Welsh slate into life, waking sympathetic murmurs, murmurs of disquiet that belonged to an era of long ago. The past. She would put on her heels once she was in her office. Her runners would go into her satchel for later. With runners on her feet no one heard her approaching. It was no wonder they called them sneakers.

She knew there was no one in the building but herself, or the card would not have been still in the door. Joseph Bayer would have removed it. At the second landing she turned to her left. Joseph was late. He was getting on in years and his wife was not well. Fran liked Joseph. His presence reassured her whenever she was feeling vulnerable. She knew that she did not belong. Was it even possible nowadays to truly *belong* anywhere? Surely Joseph also felt this disconnection? She had never spoken of it with him. Their liking for each other was due to the way they each remained reliably within the bounds of their duties, wasn't it? Their liking was instinctive. The caretaker and the scholar. The unlikely friendship making it more secure. She was comfortable with Joseph about the place. With some of the male teaching staff she was not comfortable. She did not work back in the evening if Eric Thornton had a late class. And there were others she had learned to avoid.

As she turned to her left at the head of the stairs she was met by the night chill, the upper corridor ahead of her now, the row of cell doors closed. It was a chill that resisted the warmth of the human presence. It had resisted the warmth even of the previous fierce Victorian summer when they'd had several days in a row over forty degrees. The world warming while the loony bin remained cold. Sanjeev's door, number one, the first on the left at the head of the stairs, was closed. When Sanjeev was there, his door was always open, friendly

and inviting, banishing the ghosts. His hail in the morning
was a lovely relief to hear, a splash of sunlight in the gloomy
corridor. Sanjeev was sure he belonged. He was confidently a
citizen of the world and carried within himself a steady calm,
assured by the certainty of a belief in something like reincar-
nation. Sanjeev was gracious. Was it his religion that gave him
his inner assurance? His belief in something greater than all
this? Fran was not sure what name his religion went by, but
it spared him, she knew, many questions and uncertainties of
the kind that tormented her.

There were sixteen heavy timber doors on each side of
the long corridor. The doors were freshly painted in the dark
high-gloss green required by the people charged with the
responsibility for preserving the heritage values of the institution. Why preserve those values? Things had changed, hadn't
they? This place was no longer a loony bin. The heritage of
those old days no longer needed celebrating, did it? Why look
back at it? Surely forgetting was sometimes more important
than remembering. Weren't we all doing our best to get rid
of those old values? Weren't those old hierarchies condemned
by the inclusive values of today? Why remind ourselves of how
separate we all were then? Dagoes, Poms, Abos, Aussies, Slopes,
and the one superior caste of native-born whites? The air then

heavy with contempt for the *other*. Was that heritage? Was that what we were holding on to with this dark green paint?

The doors were all closed. Sanjeev was the only member of her staff who had his own reasons for wishing to be out here in the far suburbs. The others only came to do their teaching hours before scuttling back to their offices at the city campus. Sanjeev's private business interests were here. He, alone among the staff, was more connected to the north and its culture than to the old established Anglo culture of the eastern suburbs. Sanjeev thrived in the north. The others were afraid to transfer from the city campus and clung to their offices of glass and steel, reassured by the cheerful river and the bustle of the Southbank cafes. Afraid they would become cultural outcasts if they made the north their focus. So they ignored the vice-chancellor's order to advance into the north. It was he, the black-haired Irishman, more English than he was ever Irish, who was the architect of this vision to share the benefits of education with the children of the new migrations, scarcely one of whom had sufficient English to write a decent email. Fran had told her staff, 'It is part of the price we must be willing to pay for our vision.' But they didn't have a vision. It was she who'd had a vision. They just wanted to be left alone to cross Princes Bridge for coffee or slip into Bourke Street Mall between classes to look for a new top in Myer or David Jones or in one of the little boutiques, shops that you could tell at a glance had no real future.

The vice-chancellor had discovered he was powerless to coerce them. It was he who had instructed the Dean of Studies to appoint a woman to the position of head of the new management school. 'Dr Egan will do it!' He shouted down the doubters. He needed a woman for the job, for the appearance of the thing, for his own record. At heart he was a brigand. A beast from the past, content with the narrow old hierarchies. They were cowed by him, but they did not obey him. He cared nothing for their colonial history. He swept questions of history aside and relied upon his own misguided beliefs in something older. The old suited him better than the new. He saw the grand nineteenth-century buildings in their established grounds and imagined a fine college at home in Belfast. He failed to understand that he lacked the gift of leadership for such an enterprise, or to see the faltering commitment of his staff to such an ideal, or to notice the absence of any interest among the local community for a School of Management. Like the little boutiques in the city centre, the university of the north was an enterprise created to fail. Cultural change was beyond him. The locals had no use for a university. Life was good for them as it was. He hadn't noticed that the migrants were in control and were happy about it. They had succeeded without a university. In their view, that old pile of brick and stone up there on the hill should be bulldozed and the blocks released to young first-home builders. Do something useful for a change, why don't you!

Fran reached her office. Cell number sixteen, at the far end of the corridor on the left-hand side. The last door before the great stone bulkhead of the eastern wall of the building. Out of the way of the stair landing and through traffic. She had chosen it for herself when she was allocating the offices. She had walked along the corridor looking into each of the cells on the eastern side, and when she reached number sixteen she went in and stood looking out the window, a narrow view over the roofs of the suburb spreading across the rural landscape below. It felt right; she was the princess in the tower high above the houses of the town, looking out from her window in the wall of the castle. 'I'm in my fortress,' Fran had told Tom that night. Her decision was made. She knew she could not then choose one of the other cells without doing violence to her instincts. That the windows of the other cells would also have the same view she had seen from the window of number sixteen did not impress her as an argument for changing her mind. Cell sixteen had chosen her. Some things were as they were and that was that. On this, at least, she and her mother were in agreement. It was dangerous to challenge your fate. You knew some things without evidence or reason.

She set down her satchel and got out her keys, unlocked the door and went in. She left the door open. The single three-barred window at the far end overlooking the car park below—the bars, as with the dark green paint of the doors, retained for period authenticity when the renovations were done. She put her satchel on her chair and went and stood at the narrow window. Cars had begun pulling in to the car park below. Voices floating up to her. Beyond the car park the wider reach of old pines and the open parkland of the grounds. Beyond that, the roofs of the suburb, following the contour of the hillside before flattening out in the valley. In the distance, the cold grey paddocks lost in the wintry day where cattle grazed and belts of native forest survived. The chill wind from the Antarctic was shaking the sturdy Scots pines. The pines had stood there unchallenged for a hundred and fifty years. They were showing their age. A chainsaw would take them down in less than an hour. Then they will exist as shadows in old photographs, as we shall ourselves, all of us shadows, ghosts, like the inhabitants of this place. It had begun to rain, small drops hitting the glass. She didn't know what to think sometimes. Her mother said, It's beyond me. And left it at that. And it was. Beyond her. She, her mother, had possessed a certainty to return to. A sense of home. The village of Ballyragget. The home of the Egans. She had not been able to pass it on, that sense of a home somewhere that would have you back. Something had broken between the generations. It was no use to Fran.

She turned from the window and went to her desk. She took off her overcoat then reached for the hanger on the hook beside the door and slipped the shoulders of her coat over it. She placed the hanger back on the hook and smoothed the coat's soft front. She loved her coat. Then she sat at the desk and removed her sneakers, got her heels out of her satchel and put them on. The shoes were cold. She put the warm sneakers in the satchel and set it beside the desk. She took out her laptop and opened it.

There were seventy-eight new emails. Her eyes betrayed her and searched, but there was no email from him. There had never been an email from him. There never would be an email from him, Professor Jargal Batu. She *saw* his name even though it would never be there. He might be her lifeline, mightn't he? Her anchor. One word from him. A reassurance. It's all right. There's no need to worry. She was ready to believe.

They had known they would not contact each other. Jargal Batu. Which part was his family name? They had not called each other by name. They had made no plans. He was married with a daughter. He too was organised with his life. Father, husband, professional. She knew that much. She hadn't wanted to know more. To preserve the purity of its simplicity was essential. Detail would render it sordid. But still her eyes looked for his name. When he left her in the room on the third floor of the hotel opposite the market in Hefei that morning, she had *felt* the touch of his departure in her belly. Thinking of him, she felt it now. That touch for which there is no word but only a music. The click of the hotel room door closing. Her most delicate nerve. They had not spoken. It was the level of their respect. She had watched him moving in the half-light of the room. There had been between them no word of farewell. When he was gone, she had closed her eyes and believed in the warmth of his body on the sheet beside her naked thigh, the faint perfection of his smell lingering, his lips on her scar. She was vulnerable to her vivid memory of his beauty, to the overpowering moment when he and she became one. It was another world, and they had inhabited it together, just for a moment. Forever.

The identification was on her office door: *Dr Frances Egan, Head of School.* It had been her dream year, 2001. Her *Wunderjahr.* She was appointed head of school and published four papers, all of which drew praise and attention from colleagues in Australia and favourable comment in two prestigious journals in the States and one in the UK. That year Fran's doctoral work was also successfully published as a book. As any fool might have, she had looked forward to becoming something of a celebrity in her field. She had looked forward to having *Professor Frances Egan* on her door. She had believed in it all then. Her career. That world. The perfect job and the perfect family. She had done it, hadn't she? She had beaten the curse.

The world before China. Already it was difficult to remember the confidence with which she had approached her life then. Little Tommy in his room bent over his table writing his secret stories. Margie becoming a young woman. Tom struggling to remain true to his dream of being a craftsman. Caving in and buying the electric planer when the retired surgeon and her husband asked him to make a dining suite for them from native timber. Of course, it all still mattered to her. How could it not matter to her? But now it was like an old photograph that had been folded and refolded. Not torn, not irreparably damaged. Not erased, but creased, a line across the centre of the image deforming its detail, insisting on the failure of continuity. The break.

She needed a coffee. She pushed back her chair and stood up. She walked down to the tearoom, her heels striking the old slate with their sharp hammer blows. *Here she comes!*

Phoebe Lyons and Allison Brown were there. They said hi and Fran said hi back at them and she stood at the machine and made coffee. They were silent. Interrupted. She felt them waiting for her to leave. 'See you.'

'See you, Fran.'

* * *

All morning the sound of people arriving and leaving along the corridor. The repeated slam of the front door downstairs booming through the stairwell. Young voices calling. Silences. Sudden gusts of laughter from the tearoom. The rain had set in. The drops larger and more persistent. She stayed in at lunchtime and tried to catch up with the emails.

Tom rang at quarter past one. 'I just thought I'd call.' He sounded a bit down.

Was he thinking of her stumbling on the loose stone that morning? Tom was a worrier. Was he holding something back?

She asked him, 'How's the table coming along?'

'I'm not sure the red gum's going to work for them.'

They didn't have much to say.

'Little Tommy didn't go to school.'

'Is he all right?'

'He said he thought he was getting an asthma attack. I let him stay home.'

There was a long silence. She was looking at the calendar on her desk. There was a picture of an apple orchard in spring.

'I love you,' he said.

'I love you too, darling.'

They hung up.

She stayed at her desk all afternoon, still catching up on emails. She would never catch up, of course. By the following morning the tide would be in again. She kept at it. Dogged, bored, saddened by the endless trivia. She looked at her diary for the following day: *8 am staff meeting.* It would mean leaving home before the children were up. *Matters to be discussed: induction of new faculty member; cooperative education, a new model needed; discounts for staff to allow for research, admin, grant writing, supervision; course leadership; codes of conduct; quality assurance; prepare for enrolment sessions; timetabling; conference funding policy; overseas travel to offshore campuses.*

How many times had they met over these issues? How much talk had there been? How many plans and expressions of hopes? The steady erosion of her vision. And after it all, here they were, covering the same issues yet again. Nothing done. No one cared. No one *really* cared. The culture of the university decayed and no one objected. Not seriously. Everyone complained. Complaint was the only thing they had left in common. No one cared enough to risk their job. How to bring about cultural change without personal sacrifice?

Her report to the dean and the international office on her trip to promote the residential executive short courses to the Chinese was only in note form so far. Skänder was pushing her for it and the international office was pushing him. They weren't interested in teaching their students; they just wanted the Chinese money. Lots of it. The Chinese would never provide enough to satisfy them.

She sat looking out the door into the corridor, her diary open on her lap. She could quit. She was a free woman, wasn't she?

No, she wasn't a free woman. How would she fill her days? What would they do for money? And what of that other world? He and she might travel together by Bactrian camel across the deserts of Mongolia. She would learn his language. They would discover the haunts of snow leopards. They would hold hands and brew tea and make love in the evening at their camp, the whisper of the desert wind.

Her mobile was ringing. It was still in her bag. She fished it out. Cynthia Cousins sounded shaky. 'I've got a viral infection with rheumatism. I need to go into hospital for a procedure. I'm not going to be able to make my nine o'clock lecture in the morning.' Cynthia sounded as if she was going to cry.

'It's all right, Cynth. I'll sort it. Don't worry. I'm sorry. I do hope you'll be better soon. Are you in pain?' She knew Cynthia lived with her dog on her own in a rented apartment in town. She was on a contract and feared becoming unemployed. 'Have you got someone to look after your dog?'

'My regular doctor's away for six weeks! The whole system's fucked, Fran!' Cynthia was sobbing now.

'It's just not fair, is it?'

After she got off the phone, Fran remembered she had to call Occupational Health and Safety about an anti-discrimination claim for Seda Tateossian which had been going on forever. She needed to speak with HR again for advice. And she'd done nothing about the e-commerce unit the dean had asked her to look into organising. If she didn't put things in her diary, they dropped out of her memory . . . Cynthia was right. The whole system was fucked.

The building was quiet now. Classes were finished for the day. The staff had gone home, or back to the city campus. Fran was alone. She was marking a master's thesis that was long overdue. The silence of the building had intensified into the abandonment of evening. The feeling of a presence was with her in the cell now, a sense that someone was watching and listening. What were they waiting for? The darkness of the wet sky outside seeping into the cell. The steady sound of rain driven against the window. The author of the thesis had gone back to Kuala Lumpur. He had submitted the draft electronically. Fran hated reading onscreen and had printed it out. She was sitting side-on to her desk, her back to the open door, the manuscript loose in a folder resting on her knees. She was making notes in the margins of the pages with the Visconti fountain pen Tom had given her. When she reached the end of each A4 page she placed it face down on her desk. The draft was long and intricate, with numerous detailed addenda, including graphs and charts whose complicated designs were the invention of the student. Its subject: *The formative relations of teams and technology within the organisations of small firms.*

Fran realised she had not taken in a word of what she'd read for the last two or three pages. She was feeling the cold and wondered if she should put on her overcoat. She picked up the previous two pages from her desk and began to re-read them. The section was headed: *5.3 Small Business in the North and West of Melbourne.*

Although often stereotyped as unpleasant, unattractive and polluted, Melbourne's western region has made a major contribution to the prosperity of Melbourne (Vines, 1990).

The cold was beginning to bite into her lower back. Her eyes were tired. She wondered if she would soon need glasses. Her mother had worn reading glasses from the age of fourteen. Her mother said, A boy threw sand in my eyes. As Fran read through the two pages again, she was remembering the words she had recorded in her diary that morning before getting dressed: *The sense of unease or even horror in a place where terrible things have happened is familiar to me.* She had goosebumps on her forearms. She could not imagine what it must have been like to have been locked in this cell for the night, night after night, for years; the cold, the loneliness, the haunted oppression of the stone silence, the heaviness of the walls, an impenetrable existence.

There was a shared ward in the old days, when the campus was a lunatic asylum. The ward was in a room on the ground floor, a room now used for academic staff meetings. *For Convict Lunatics* was written in a beautiful copperplate hand in old browned ink on the framed original hand-drawn plan of the institution. The large, detailed plan hung on a wall in the basement, a long windowless gallery once used as the mortuary, now the student cafeteria. It was said the death rate among the inmates of the asylum each year was on average ten per cent. The drawing of the plan was highly accomplished. When she first saw it, Fran was fascinated by its commitment to detail and saw in it an attempt to achieve perfection, the expression of a need for total control. Control of something the authorities feared, the lunatic and the criminal—those individuals, in other words, who refused to abide by the rules of the establishment. The ones who couldn't take it any longer, the ones who stepped out of line and screamed in your face. Without rules, lunacy might infect the whole of society. Suicide, adultery, things like that. The criminal act? Was adultery a crime in those days? A threat to the sacred family? The family, the unit on which the civilised system of the world is based. She took a deep breath and eased her shoulders. Stealing, that was particularly hated. And what about murder? The wilful killing of a fellow human being. At today's rate, one woman a week killed by her husband or partner. One a week! It was impossible to think of Tom ever threatening her or the children with physical violence. Tom did not have it in him to be a violent man. He would put his head in his hands and weep if she were to tell him of the bliss of her naked hours with Professor Jargal Batu in the hotel room in Hefei. But he would not strike her. Wouldn't his tears be worse than being struck by him?

In law the definition of lunacy had been entirely subjective: *Such mental unsoundness as interferes with civil rights or transactions.* Who, in the deadly hierarchy of men's authority, got to decide which of us were the unsound ones? And what sort of transactions? Any sort? All sorts? Business? Personal? Professional? Who decided? What had the woman who had occupied this cell done to make them decide she was crazy? Was she an adulteress of unsound mind? Did ecstasy in a hotel room in the Chinese city of Hefei count as lunacy? Of course, they didn't call it lunacy now. But did anything real change when the men in charge changed the words they used to describe whatever it was they meant? The nut case. The crazy fucker. The one who would not stand still when told to? The wild roamer dashing around senselessly doing unsound things?

When she first saw that drawing of the institution, Fran's reaction was to doubt if there was anyone today with the skill to make such a drawing with pen and ink and without the help of a computer. Time had darkened it and given to it an elusive, even a romantic quality it would not have possessed when it was fresh and new. The drawing, like old wine, had matured with time and taken on characteristics it had not had when it was first made. Romance. Now its anonymity in past time lent to it a sense of mystery. The number of places reserved for convict lunatics was twelve, so the legend read. A small number compared to the accommodation dedicated to *Refractory Females*: three hundred and forty, the most numerous category in the whole plan. What did a woman have to do to qualify as refractory? What did it mean, refractory? Stubborn, unmanageable, resistant to authority. Isn't that all of us now? Aren't we all of unsound mind? Haven't we all become refractory females? Dangerous lunatic women, flying about the place at liberty, trampling authority underfoot, overturning the old order. No longer named lunatic, renamed revolutionary. The revolution of the refractory women. She heard herself laugh. Was that it? Open the door of the cage and jump out.

The thesis was slipping from her lap. She grabbed it.

After the official opening of the campus, once the local press had taken their photographs and driven back to the city, she had traipsed around with the minister and the little knot of VIPs during their inspection of the buildings. She was one of them, herself an honorary member of the leadership cohort, as was the Irishman, the vice-chancellor, the man with the so-called vision of cultural change for the north. He had, he claimed that day, been inspired by a visiting Australian colleague to his home in Belfast who had shown him a photograph of the impressive old buildings, abandoned then and unused. It was his vision that had endowed the great complex with its new purpose. They had paused in front of the plan hanging on the wall in the cold basement, where the corpses of the naked lunatics had once been laid out, corpse shapes under white sheets, she could see them. Why were they naked? Naked, they were stripped of the last remnant of human dignity left to them after they had been classified lunatic. Who in this world would not dread to see a loved one brought to such an end? Carlos Skänder, the Dean of Studies, was leading the group around and had paused them in front of the plan to explain the impressive layout of the vast complex of buildings, pointing with the stubby forefinger of his left hand first to this building then to another. Did anyone follow him?

A sudden loud crack in the roof timbers above her head made Fran jump. She looked at her watch. She had forgotten the time. Her train was due in seven minutes. She wasn't going to make it. She said, 'Fuck!' The next train scheduled to stop at Castlemaine didn't leave Sunbury for another hour and a half. She called Tom and told him she would be late. 'Don't wait for dinner. I'll make myself scrambled eggs when I get home.'

'Just be careful driving home from the station in this rain. It's a filthy night. We need you here in one piece.'

She sat a moment, gathering her resolve to return to the thesis. Her brain was dry, numb, crumbly, its fibres unable to carry messages of poetry or love. Thinking of him induced in her a state of torment. She resisted for a minute or two longer, then she reached under her skirt and touched the scar on the inside of her left thigh. Lightly at first, as lightly with the soft pad of her index finger as he had caressed it with his lips. Above her the timbers of the old roof groaned. The building was past its use-by date. She straightened her skirt. Some part of the great structure adjusting, the audible process of decay. Small sounds creating the depth of silence and weight within which she was embedded, her vulnerable body, beyond which lay her own transience in this world. How sad it all is, she thought.

She made an effort to focus on the task at hand and read on, further into the barren landscape of the thesis.

Had that exquisite night with him opened for her a way to live beyond the mundane? Had she seen in that hotel room in Hefei a vision of possibility far beyond the narrow horizons of her own contented mediocrity? A previously unvisited potential within herself beyond the trivial realities of her days? Was she wasting her life? Just that once she had stepped through the door and seen it. She had *known* it. It was in her now. *He* was within her, his beauty, his calm, his deep steadiness denoting an inner certainty she could share with no one else, claiming a reality grander than her own. His mystery. Her own mystery. No, she would not forget him. Never! She was tormented by the question that the experience might have made a return to life within the mundane impossible for her. This question terrified her. Surely she did not have the courage for it? She dreaded to be faced with its challenge. It was a cliff. Did others have to make the leap? It was final. Were she ever to jump, her beautiful children, her family, they could not survive it. Little Tommy without his mother? It was unthinkable. How was she ever to compose herself and find once again the simple peace of her old contentment? But had she ever really been content? Contentment was a myth. She had striven for her goals, for her vision of herself. Contentment was never hers. Her mother called her 'the difficult one' for a reason. Tom, too, had known no measure of contentment in his wife. But she would still like to trust in the lie of her old contentment. To lie is, after all, to create a small place of some comfort and safety amid the turmoil.

She focused on the words on the page in front of her.

The association was tested by examination of the
correlations between the items relating to training,
rewards, flexibility and culture with the statement of
improved effectiveness, Item 16. The correlations are
presented in Table 6.7

The crash of the outer door closing downstairs boomed
through the empty building and Fran jumped. Loose pages
from the thesis slipped from her knees and fell to the floor.
She waited to hear whoever it was coming up the stairs. She
was hoping to God it wasn't Eric Thornton on the prowl. The
silence settled. The stillness. Someone was in the building with
her. She listened, holding her breath. She should have been
safely on the train on the way home by now. There was the
puzzling sound of a sudden rapid pattering on the slate in
the corridor outside, then Joseph's little white terrier, Jenny,
skidded into the room. The small dog stood and shook the
rain from its coat, then raced from corner to corner, checking
for interesting smells. Joseph helloed softly from the passage.
Fran set the thesis aside on her desk and bent down to collect
the loose pages from the floor.

'I'm sorry to disturb you, Dr Egan,' Joseph said. He was
standing in the doorway looking down at her. 'I saw your light
was still on up here as I was crossing the car park. I thought
you must have forgotten to turn it off.'

Fran straightened and set the pages on the open folder of the thesis. She stood and brushed at her skirt. 'You're not disturbing me, Joseph.'

He was wearing his old brown felt hat with its misshapen brim and the ancient pale mackintosh that carried the story of its past in the motley stains that no amount of dry-cleaning was ever going to get rid of. Joseph was out of breath from climbing the stairs. The faint smell of cigarettes on him.

Fran said, 'I missed my train. I'm so glad to see you.' She reached out and touched the sleeve of his mackintosh, touching something safe and familiar. 'You're soaked.' They looked at each other and both of them smiled.

'I will dry off,' he said.

He was tall, a man in his middle sixties. A little stooped from years of physical work. His old clothes had once been stylish and still gave him a look of seriousness.

She said, 'Please sit down and catch your breath.'

'Thank you.'

He seated himself in her chair.

She said, 'Take off your mac. You'll catch a cold.'

'It is weatherproof.'

She laughed. 'But you're not.'

He was a smoker. She liked the smell of cigarette smoke on him. She rested her buttocks against the edge of the desk and looked at him. He was still a handsome man. Distinguished even. He might have been a scholar in another life, a more settled life somewhere. Why had he become a caretaker? What had happened? His little dog, Jenny, came and sat beside him and began to nibble one of its feet. Joseph coughed into his hand.

She asked him, 'Would you like a drink of water?'

'No, no, thank you, Dr Egan.' He waved his hand, dismissing her offer.

They were silent. It was not an uncomfortable silence. A minute passed, then another, Jenny nuzzling her feet. Fran noticed that Joseph had long slim fingers.

She said, 'I sometimes feel a presence in this office. Do you know what I mean? Other people have felt it. It's not just me.' When he didn't respond she went on. 'I've wondered what it is we're aware of when we have the feeling someone is with us and we know very well we are alone.'

Joseph coughed, clearing the phlegm from his throat. He hesitated, looking up at her and considering her. 'Is it a good idea for you to be sitting up here all on your own for the next hour or two? Eleni and I would be delighted if you would join us for a cup of tea. I have something I think will interest you, Dr Egan. I've been hoping for a chance to show it to you since before you went to China.'

'A cup of tea would be lovely, Joseph. Call me Fran.' She stood away from the desk and reached for her overcoat. 'What can it possibly be that you want to show me? How exciting.'

Joseph stood waiting for her while she gathered the pages of the thesis together and put them in her satchel with her laptop. He was looking down at his little dog, the dog looking up at him. He might have been speaking to the dog when he said, 'If we said we had seen a ghost, people might think we also believed in the devil.' Jenny put her head on one side and gave a little shake, agreeing with him. 'And then they would ridicule us for our superstitions. So we find a neutral word and say presence.' He laughed softly. 'But we mean ghost all the same. Don't we?' Jenny looked at Fran.

'I suppose you're right,' Fran said. Her inclination also was to address Jenny. 'I definitely feel something here that I don't feel in other places. But I really don't believe in ghosts. The feeling that there is someone here with me makes me uneasy but it doesn't frighten me. Does Jenny feel the presence of ghosts? There are plenty of them in this place.'

Joseph said, 'Perhaps we should ask her.'

Jenny ran on ahead of them while Fran locked the door, then she and Joseph walked together along the corridor. Fran said, 'Don't you think when we change the name of something, we also change what we mean? Don't we change the name of something because we no longer think it's what we once thought it was?'

Joseph said nothing to this. When they were going down the stairs into the foyer, and as if he was talking to himself, or perhaps saying something just to get it said rather than saying it in order to re-engage Fran in the conversation, he said, 'Sometimes we're mistaken when we discard old meanings. We might be discarding the truth of them.'

Fran thought this might well be true. The truths of her mother were not her own, after all. Or so she had always believed. Perhaps one day she would understand why her mother had gone home to Ireland. It wasn't just a longing to recapture something of her own early life, was it? I'll never be anything but an Irish woman in my heart, she said, trying to explain herself. I've tried for your father's sake to be an Australian. But I'm not one. I'm always going to be a stranger here. Now he's gone, I don't want to die among strangers. My old people are lying in the ground in the cemetery at Donaghmore and that's where I'll be lying myself. Alongside them. It was all a matter of her belief. Fran didn't have it. Fran didn't have a lot of patience, either, with her mother at the time. We're your people, too, and it's us you're leaving. They didn't get anywhere with it. When they parted at the airport her mother turned to her at the last minute and said, I love you, darling. And Fran was moved and said back to her, And I love you too, Mum. And she stood and waved her off. And neither of them was dry-eyed. It was then, she remembered, once her mother had gone and it was too late to say anything, standing there alone in the airport, that she saw the deeper truth of her mother's inability to love her when she was a child: not all women are born to be mothers. It was a simple enough idea, once you accepted it. It was not a failure in her mother, as Fran had always thought it. Mother love, after all, was not a necessary endowment of womanhood. Being a mother had not suited her. Why should it have? Fran remembered turning around and walking out of the airport and going in search of her car in the vast sea of cars. She wanted to tell her mother, It's all right. Everything's all right. I hope I haven't made you feel guilty.

She followed Joseph around behind the stairs. He opened the back door and stood aside to let her go through ahead of him. A rush of damp night air, like a sudden exhalation of cold breath, washed over her as she went through the open door into the night. The smell of rotted leaves and something of the old drains of the asylum days. The thought came to her that rain brings out smells from the past that have been lying dormant in the fabric of our surroundings for years, as if the past never really leaves, but finds another place to be itself.

They had entered the cloister, a long stone walkway ahead of them, the barrel-vaulted ceiling giving an ecclesiastical feel to the area, something sombre and religious. At the far end of the cloister ahead of them a soft yellow light was falling from a side window onto the flagstones. The central court-yard on their left was a void of blackness and glitter of rain. They had emerged into a part of the complex of buildings that had remained untouched by upgrades and alterations since it was built in the 1870s. They might have stepped back into old Europe, a time of stone and silence and heaviness and history, and rain. A time of the untempered sovereignty of men and religion and their categories of right and wrong. She would not have wanted to live then. They might have burned her or flayed her alive with her lover, and made a party of it in the town square. Jenny paused to lap at the water gathered in the gutter where the great square flagstones of the cloister stood a few centimetres above the broken edges of the uneven cobbles of the courtyard, her little pink tongue flicking at the puddle.

Fran walked beside Joseph's silent figure towards the distant light, along the stone way within the shelter of the vaulted ceiling, the black rain falling into the broken mirror of the courtyard. She was wondering what it was he wanted to show her. She was aware of her disordered interior life standing uncertainly against Joseph's steadiness. She envied his calm reserve, the way he managed to remain outside the hierarchies of the system that employed him. His was no ordinary response to the situation. His presence spoke to her of values altogether finer, and more durable, than the threadbare values of most of her colleagues. He seemed to want for nothing. This had been her earliest impression of him. She was certain Joseph knew himself accountable for his actions; they—Skänder and his mob—would never be held accountable for the failure they were creating. They would walk away with their bonuses and go off and destroy something else and none of it would touch their consciences.

They drew level with the lighted window at the end of the cloister. Joseph opened the door beside the window and he went in and stepped to one side. Fran followed him into a warmly lit living room, the smell of stale tobacco smoke in the air. A wood fire was burning in the hearth. Before the hearth a black-and-white cat lay curled up asleep in the centre of a blue-and-white rug. Jenny ran across the room and tried to nudge the cat aside, but the cat resisted, tucking in its backside and giving out a low growl. Jenny abandoned the attempt to shift the cat and lay down beside it, pressing her body against it. A woman sitting in an armchair on the far side of the fire was struggling to rise from her chair.

Joseph said, 'Dr Egan's going to have a cup of tea with us. She has missed her train.' He did not introduce the woman or offer to help her out of her chair but went across the room and out through a door at the back.

Fran went over to the woman. 'Please don't get up.'

The woman waved her away with an impatient gesture. 'I'm getting up!' She reached for a heavy black stick that was lying across an untidy pile of newspapers and books on the low table in front of her. She grasped the stick and swung it out and stood, leaning her weight unsteadily on the large black knob of the head of the sturdy weapon, the skin over the backs of her hands tensed, a map of heavy veins, a world of old age. She controlled the tremor and stood as still as a sentry, swaying slightly, examining Fran. After a moment or two she nodded. 'Hm! So, you're beautiful. He didn't tell me. Did he tell you I'm his wife?' She spoke flatly, without expression, with a strong accent. 'I'm his Eleni.' She laughed.

'You have a lovely cosy home here.'

'You think so? There's no garden. It's not ours. Your university includes it in what they cunningly call Joseph's *package*, so they can reduce his salary by the amount of the rent. It was their idea, not ours. We will be here until they decide they have no more use for him. Take off your coat and warm yourself. He'll be out in a minute. You're cold. You look tired. Looking tired suits you. Beautiful women are more beautiful when they are tired.'

Fran took off her overcoat and laid it over the back of the easy chair which stood on the other side of the low table from Eleni's seat. She placed her satchel on the floor beside it and sat down. Eleni stood watching her, not saying anything, her expression as empty of emotion as her voice had been. Fran looked up at her and smiled. She was a little apprehensive. Eleni had obviously decided that being old and frail entitled her to speak her mind. Fran watched her going through an elaborate series of motions to regain her seat. With a heavy sigh she settled herself.

'Did he tell you I'm dying?' She didn't wait for Fran to respond but went on. 'We met here.' She looked directly at Fran. 'I was a patient. Yes. You're surprised. I was one of the loonies.' She chuckled. 'With me it was the torment of the voices. My Joseph was one of the gardeners in those days. He was a beautiful young man. When they took us locked-ward crazies out for a walk I saw him. He was squatting, his fingers digging into the earth. He stood up and looked at me and we fell in love. It was as simple as that. Joseph saved me. The voices struggled against his love, and they lost. His love silenced them. I don't know what I did to deserve him. He asked Mr Cool to speak to the director, and I was re-examined and pronounced cured. They said, We cured you! But it was Joseph. My beloved man. We were married in the chapel here. I would have preferred a real church. We were happy. For many years we were happy. When you are old you can no longer be happy. Did your mother tell you that? I hope you are happy. Now's the time for you to be happy. Tragically happy, like the old Greeks. My beautiful sad people. Are you married, Dr Egan? Do you have children? We have never had a child. We wanted children. I prayed to the Almighty but he was pitiless and refused me. There is nowhere here for me to sit in the sun. Without the sun the soul of a Greek is in mourning. Now I am old and dying and I am tired of the struggle. I will be happy to go. My only regret is that Joseph will be alone. He has Jenny. And his package, they call it.' She stared steadily at Fran, her eyes narrowed, inflamed around the rims, watery. She was concentrating. She was not wearing glasses. 'My Joseph is not a birthday present.' She laughed. 'A package! That's my Joseph. They can go to hell. And they will. Joseph and I will be together again in heaven. Are you a believer? Do you teach your children so that they will believe? It's the least you can do for them. Without God we're nothing. We're just rubbish without the grace of our Lord. Teach them to believe! Or they will curse you in their old age. Children become old people. You don't know that yet. You will find it out. One day you will look in the mirror and that beautiful woman will no longer look back at you. One day it will be an old stranger who looks back at you from the mirror. And then your sad time will begin. It will come like a messenger in the night and take the blessing of your life and lay the curse of old age on you. And if you don't believe in Him, what will you be then? Eh? What then, Professor Egan?' She laughed and coughed.

Fran was sitting forward on the chair, holding her hands out to the warmth of the wood fire. She was trying to picture Eleni as the beautiful and troubled young woman who fell in love with Joseph, but she couldn't. Old age and youth were too different. She didn't say anything because she wasn't able to think of an appropriate way of responding to Eleni's way of speaking to her. Also, Eleni spoke as if she didn't expect a response. Fran watched her now as she extended the heavy stick and hooked a piece of firewood from the pile then bent and picked it up and threw it into the flames. The dog gave a start then settled again.

Fran and Joseph's wife sat gazing into the flames, the cracking and spitting of the protesting wood. The warmth of the fire, the quiet in the settled room, the hiss of rain outside, the sleeping animals. The two women waiting for Joseph to return. The piece of split red gum Eleni had tossed into the fire shifted and sent up a spray of crackling sparks. Fran thought of a last sad little demonstration of resistance to the consuming fire.

She saw that the older woman had her eyes shut. Her brief outpouring of questions and disclosures seemed to have drained her. The firelight flowered in her cheeks, her dry grey hair falling about her face, strands escaping from the black elastic tie with which she had bound it, her heavy body leaning sideways. Her mouth firmly clamped in a hard thin line, her strong jaw clamped, as if she resisted an impulse to speak her thoughts, holding the voices behind the barrier, at which they were clamouring to be heard like a crowd of refugees at the wire. Eleni was not asleep. She was closed. The burning wood cracked loudly and she flinched but didn't open her eyes. Fran saw a dying woman who was remembering being young and in love.

The door at the back of the room opened and Joseph came in. He was carrying a blue plastic tray with teapot and milk jug, sugar bowl and three china mugs. There was a packet of Arnott's ginger nut biscuits. He had changed into a pair of dark trousers and a brown sweater with a roll neck. Fran had never seen him wearing these clothes before. The trousers, pinstriped, old and shiny, were from what had once been a business suit. She thought of the empty trouser legs of the beggar in the Hefei market. Joseph looked like an old lawyer from Collins Street who had been a friend of her father's when she was a little girl. The lawyer was a man who seemed to her then to have been forever the same old man, a person not subject to the changes around him. Seeing him entering the house to pay a visit to her father, she had believed she herself stood outside of time as he did. She knew in those far-off days that she would remain a child forever. It saddened her a little to realise now that she had forgotten the name of her father's friend. He must have died long ago. Did anyone remember him?

Fran made room for the tray among the scatter of newspapers and books that covered the low table in front of her. Joseph placed the tray on the table and straightened. There was a picture of two galahs on the tray, their beaks touching as if they were kissing. As Joseph straightened, he pulled a small notebook from the back pocket of his trousers. He placed the notebook on the table beside the tray. The binding of the little book was dark, stained and curled at the corners, as if it had been left out in the weather.

Joseph turned away and fetched an upright chair from the dining table in the centre of the room and set it down in front of the low table. He sat. 'Do you have milk and sugar, Dr Egan?'

'Just black, thanks, Joseph.' Fran saw that Eleni was watching her, the hint of a sardonic smile in the old woman's pale eyes, as if she asked, Well, Dr Egan, so what do you think might be the point of all this then?

When he had served them both tea, Joseph picked up the damaged notebook and held it out to Fran. 'I think this will interest you. It belonged to the last patient to occupy your office.'

Fran took the little book in her hand. 'Oh, thank you, Joseph. How fascinating.' She opened the book. The pages were covered with small neat handwriting.

Joseph said, 'Valerie Sommers was an inmate here. She occupied your office for five years. From 1957 until the facility was closed in 1962. In Valerie's time the lunatic asylum was renamed the Caloola Mental Hospital. You asked me if we change the meaning when we change the name. We always want to soften things. We want to evade the hard truth. The new name helps us to conceal the truth from ourselves. This place became a hospital instead of an asylum for lunatics. I don't know if the patients noticed a difference. Perhaps some of their relatives were glad to know that the world thought their loved ones patients and no longer lunatics.'

Fran held the small notebook. It felt at once like an intimate object. She was moved by Joseph's evident pleasure in showing it to her. He smiled when he caught her eye. It was something real between them.

'Yes,' he said. 'You may keep it. I'm giving it to you. But it's not mine to give. Who else could own it now? The real owner is no longer with us. Out of all the cells you might have chosen for your office, you chose Valerie's. I noticed at once, the very day you came here. Your choice of her room meant something that I found interesting. And you have felt her presence there with you and you are not afraid of her. Ever since you settled in there last year, I have hoped for the right moment to give you her book.' His gaze shifted to the notebook in her lap. 'I believe she would have wanted you to have it.'

On an impulse, Fran stood up and leaned over to kiss Joseph on the cheek. 'Thank you, Joseph!'

She sat down again. She realised she was blushing.

As if the little scene delighted her, Eleni said, 'You see, Joseph! Now you have embarrassed Dr Egan. She's in love with you.' She let out a loud jarring cackle then bent forward, coughing thickly.

The sudden flush of emotion had taken Fran by surprise. To hide her confusion she opened the notebook. The name

Valerie Sommers was written at the top of the first page, and the date 12 August 1957. The pages were faintly lined in blue. The handwriting was small and neat and stayed within the lines. A sentence written across the top of the page was underlined, and was clearly intended by the writer to be the title of what followed: 'The hopelessness and the necessity of my illusions.' Was it a quote from the Old Testament? She looked up and met Joseph's gaze. 'Thank you.' It didn't seem enough.

Joseph said, 'Each of the cells upstairs, including your office, originally had a corner cupboard. The privileged inmates kept their few private belongings in them.'

Eleni said, 'That one, Valerie Sommers, was privileged all right. Her father was a friend of Caloola's chief psychiatrist, the great Doctor William Vincent-Sinclair, who blessed me and pronounced me sane enough to marry Joseph and bear his children. God of all he surveyed, that man was. Valerie's daddy was the Honourable Sir Arthur Sommers, the Chief Justice of the High Court of Australia when that court was in Melbourne. Vincent-Sinclair never received a knighthood and couldn't help hating the judge for getting one. Vincent-Sinclair wanted to be recognised as a great man too, like his old friend. But there. He was overlooked, wasn't he? He was never to meet the King. Poor fellow!' She coughed and drank some tea. 'So there! Privileged. Your Valerie was not like my lot down there in the barracks with our tormentors.' She laughed. 'Joseph knows. He saved me. Ask him. He knows all about the old locked ward.' She made a sudden explosive noise, part cough, part strangle, then she rested back in her chair and closed her eyes and sighed heavily, as if she could bear no more of it.

Joseph had listened attentively while Eleni was speaking. He said softly, 'Perhaps if you take a drink of your tea, darling.'

Eleni waved her arm at him. 'Oh, shut up, for God's sake!' She coughed some more, struggling to get her breath. She tugged a handkerchief from the open front of her dress and dabbed at her eyes.

Joseph waited until she was settled before turning to Fran. 'The corner cupboards were fixtures. They were made by craftsmen in the old days from fragrant red cedar. After the closure of the facility in 1962, your part of the building remained unoccupied. I was here as an assistant gardener and general handyman. I was the only one by that time who was familiar with the workings of the old boiler and our outdated heating and plumbing arrangements. I fulfilled the duties of caretaker even then, as a boy of sixteen, though my work was largely honorary and was not officially recognised until much later. I was useful to them.'

Eleni said, 'You should tell Dr Egan about your mother.'

'I was four years of age when my mother was admitted to the asylum. She was an involuntary patient.'

'Like me,' Eleni said. 'A loony. Joseph's mother had the voices too. He understood all that.'

Joseph said, 'When my mother was admitted the authorities weren't sure what to do with me and would have sent me to a children's home.'

Eleni said, 'He means an orphanage.'

'I was fortunate to be taken into the care of the head gardener, Mr Cool, and his wife. They had no children of their own and treated me as if I were their son. They loved me. I loved them too. We were happy. Eventually they were able to adopt me officially. Without Mr Cool's help, Eleni and I would never have been allowed to marry.'

'Officially,' Eleni said, emphasising the word, as if the sound of it amused her, 'our Joseph is Mr Cool. What a pity there is no one to call him Daddy Cool.' She laughed and coughed into her handkerchief. 'No one has a sense of humour anymore. Why is that? Did we all change our diet or something? We're all po-faced with the fear of upsetting someone. Speaking out of turn has gone out of fashion. I have lived to see it. Why are we all silent? Even the voices have packed it in. Something happened. What was it? Does anybody know?'

'Mr and Mrs Cool have passed on,' Joseph said. 'When I was old enough, I was put on here as an assistant gardener, but I had always worked with Mr Cool from my school days and was happy to do it. He paid me a shilling from time to time from his own pocket. I did not get the position of assistant gardener until I was fifteen. My pay then was twenty-five shillings a week. I saved ten shillings of it.'

Eleni said, 'Dr Egan doesn't need to know what they paid you, Joseph. She's not interested in how poor you were. Everyone always thinks their own story is the most interesting one we're ever going to hear. Why don't you tell her what you want her to know?' She clamped her jaw and closed her eyes and lay back in her chair. She did not relax but lay rigidly pressed against the support of the chair back, holding herself against the onset of pain.

Joseph looked at Fran. 'I don't wish to bore you, but I have known of the existence of that notebook that is now in your hands for a long time. I knew it long before it fell from the back of the cupboard and startled me.'

Eleni opened her eyes and said with deeply pained irritation, 'Yes! Yes! But you haven't told her that yet! He doesn't tell his stories in the right order. He doesn't get his facts in their proper place. How can Dr Egan understand if you jump about from one thing to another?' She closed her eyes and murmured to herself, 'It's too much! God forgive me!'

Joseph said, 'My wife is right, of course. There is too much to tell. This place has been my life. I know its secrets. My mother is buried here. I have no memory of my father. My mother was committed in 1946, just after the end of the war. We had been in Australia a year.' As if the 1940s and 1980s were smoothly connected for him in time, Joseph went on without a pause. 'When the workmen came to do the renovations in the eighties, I went out into the yard and examined the contents of a large bin they had placed there and into which they were depositing discarded materials. It was then I discovered they were tearing out the cedar corner cupboards upstairs in your area. Many of the discarded cedar boards were broken, but there were also quite a number that I was able to save. The timber seemed to me to be deserving of being saved for future use. I have those boards. I can show them to you.'

Eleni groaned. 'For the love of God, Joseph! Dr Egan doesn't want to see timber boards!'

'The same evening, I went upstairs and looked into each cell to see if any of the cupboards had not yet been torn out by the workmen. The only one that was left intact, and which was no doubt due for destruction the following day, was in the cell that you chose for your office, Valerie Sommers' old cell, the last in the row, number sixteen. I was able to remove the cupboard without destroying it. When I removed it, I remember well that despite its great age the wood still gave off the lovely perfume of its oils.' He paused and pointed to the corner of the room behind his wife and to the right of the fireplace. 'There! That is your cupboard.'

Fran turned around and looked.

Eleni said wearily, as if she possessed scarcely enough energy to get the words out, 'It's not Dr Egan's cupboard. It's Valerie's cupboard. Truth is important. Just stick to the truth.'

Fran looked at the corner cupboard. 'It's lovely.'

Joseph said, 'Yes. The workmanship is fine. It was a slip of the tongue to call it your cupboard. My wife is right. Today there is nothing like it. The notebook you are holding in your hands fell to the floor when I loosened the backboard from the grip of the nails. It must have slid down into the crack between the backboard of the cupboard and the wall. I don't know whether Valerie Sommers placed it there with the intention of concealing it from the matron and the nurse supervisor, or whether she put the book there for safekeeping and was unable to get it out again. Or whether, in fact, when she left this place she forgot to retrieve it. The matron and the head nurse read everything patients wrote. For some reason that was never explained to me, the authorities were afraid of the written word and it was always reported to the director by the staff. They spoke about it in hushed tones, as if a bomb had been planted in the institution and might explode if it was spoken of in a normal voice. No matter how private it was to them, the written word of patients was always confiscated. Patients were known to find many quite astonishing ways of concealing such things from the authorities.' He coughed heavily then leaned forward and picked up his cup and drank off the remains of his tea. He breathed deeply, emitting a slight wheeze as he exhaled. 'Thinking of that day when I found the notebook reminds me of the smell also of the dust that was released when I eased the cupboard free from its anchor points, and the sudden movement of the book falling out from behind it gave me a start.'

'So now he is going to tell you,' Eleni said. 'My God!'

'It was a moment that lasted for no more than a fraction of a second, but I saw in the sudden flurry of the falling pages the agitated feathers of a bird that I supposed I had released from long captivity. Even in that tiny lapse of time, during which my mind interpreted the falling book as a bird liberated from captivity, I both believed and I didn't believe. I saw the bird, yet knew of the impossibility of its having endured for years in silent bondage behind the cupboard. I knew all this. My sensible mind knew it. But another place in my mind that was not governed by the merely sensible believed in the bird. This state of belief and disbelief happening to us at the same time may not be exactly the same as what you referred to when you said to me in your office that you believed someone—you said a presence—was with you in Valerie's cell though you knew there was no one there. But in some way, are our two experiences not similar? Are they not clear evidence that we possess two minds, one governed by rationality and the other governed by a sense that lies outside the rational? We believe, despite knowing that what we believe cannot be true. And do we not treasure our irrational beliefs more dearly than our rational ones? Our illusions are more precious to us than our knowledge. We do not readily discard our intuitive and irrational beliefs. When it comes to my illusion of the bird and your sense of a presence in your office, illusion triumphs over knowledge. Knowing is not enough for us. In order to believe, we must feel.' He fell silent and looked steadily at Fran. 'Am I right? When you feel the presence in your office while knowing you are alone, you are convinced. To feel is enough for you. I shall never forget the bird that flew out from behind the cupboard. I still feel the rush of its liberation from those long years of its captivity as if it were my own liberation I witnessed that day.' He gestured at the notebook she was holding on her lap. 'You hold my bird of liberty in your hands.'

Eleni said, 'Oh my God! His bird of liberty! Have you ever heard the like of it?'

Joseph rummaged among the jumble of papers on the table. After a moment of searching, he made a satisfied sound and pulled out a cigarette packet. He held the crumpled packet for Fran to see. 'There's one in there! Would you mind if I smoke a cigarette? I thought I was out of them.'

Fran said, 'Please! I like the smell of cigarette smoke.'

When Joseph smiled, his features were briefly transformed into those of a much younger man. Something of his youth, the wonder of those earlier years, was awakened in him by his memory of the liberated bird that stood in his mind as an emblem of his own liberty. He took the last cigarette from the crumpled packet and he reached around and picked up a box of matches from the dining table and lit the cigarette. It all took time. He drew the smoke deeply into his lungs and held it there, then slowly released it, lifting his chin and letting the smoke rise from between his lips towards the ceiling.

'You asked me,' he said, 'what that residue of feeling must be that remains in the fabric of a place long after the deed has been done. The existence of that bird remains real for me. I see it now.' He moved the papers on the low table aside to uncover a glass ashtray. 'The symbolic is real,' he said, speaking with a quiet assurance. 'We call that kind of reality sacred, because it is the thing that expresses our hopes.' There were several cigarette butts in the ashtray.

Fran wanted to hear more from Joseph. She noticed one of the butts had the faint carmine stain of lipstick on its filter. She saw how Eleni was watching him, a smile in her eyes, no doubt seeing the beautiful young Joseph who had stolen her heart and silenced for her the torment of the voices.

Eleni looked directly at Fran and said in a matter-of-fact voice, 'Those things will kill him.' Eleni's tone was faintly mocking when she said then, 'Joseph will tell you Valerie's story.' She held out her cup to him. 'Pour me another one, love.'

Joseph took his wife's cup and refilled it from the teapot. She did not take milk or sugar. He handed the cup of tea to her and she reached and took it from him, making an exaggerated kissing shape at him with her heavy lips.

He sat down again. 'Valerie was in her early thirties, perhaps only thirty-one, when her father agreed to the head psychiatrist's suggestion that she spend some time here. I was eleven at the time and was working with Mr Cool in the grounds by then. Valerie was a privileged patient and often walked in the garden. At first she was with her friend, Jessie Macdonald, an older woman. Then Jessie was sent away. After that, Valerie was always alone and would sometimes stop on the path and watch me clipping the grass around the borders of the flowerbeds or pulling weeds. She was sad in those days after her friend was sent away, but if I caught her eye on those occasions when she watched me working she would give me a smile. She carried that little book with her as if it were her prayer book and she could not be without it. I saw her from time to time on fine days sitting on the bench in the shade of the pines down there writing in that book. Sometimes she smiled to herself, and was lost in her thoughts; at other times she scowled and shouted at me to go away if she caught sight of me watching her. One day she surprised me when she came up to me and put her hand on my shoulder. She did not speak but looked at me in such a way that I believed she expressed some gentle fellow feeling for me. That she laid her hand on me was a great surprise. Her touch was approving. I was innocent and felt myself honoured. It would not be an exaggeration to say that, although we never explored our friendship in any way, Valerie Sommers and I were what people call kindred spirits. The other's existence here was important to us in a private way that we never expressed other than by these small gestures of approval, such as her hand on my shoulder.'

Eleni laughed. 'What a memory some people have. Kindred spirits! He means they were both nut cases.'

'As my wife said, Valerie's father was Sir Arthur Sommers. Mr Cool knew Sir Arthur. He was head gardener at Sir Arthur's big house before he came to the institution. Everyone called Valerie's father Sir Arthur. That was how he insisted on being known, Sir Arthur. He was proud of his knighthood, so Mr Cool said. Mr Cool liked to reminisce about the old days while he and I were eating our lunch together in some chosen spot in the grounds. Sir Arthur was the Chief Justice of the High Court and a close friend of the director, Dr Vincent-Sinclair. Vincent-Sinclair did not hide his envy of Sir Arthur very well but showed it whenever visitors commented on the great prestige enjoyed by the judge, a man honoured by the King of England. Both their families had grand houses out in Canterbury, on the hill. Mr Cool was often called upon to deliver a load of horse manure from our stables to the gardeners at Sir Arthur's home. Valerie was an only child and must have been lonely in that grand house with no playmates. She used to come out of the house sometimes and stand and watch Mr Cool unloading the horse manure, so he told me. He said he felt sorry for her. Her mother had committed suicide when Valerie was eight years of age. After that, Sir Arthur sent her to a boarding school. Some years later, when she was a senior student, she was involved in a scandal at the school with another girl and they were both expelled. No one ever spoke of it but Mr Cool knew all about it from the servants out at Sir Arthur's place. He did not tell me what had caused the scandal. Valerie, so Mr Cool said, became troubled and difficult after her expulsion from the school, and Sir Arthur sent her to England to live with his sister in London.'

Joseph drew on his cigarette and coughed.

Eleni made a strangled sound and raised her hands in the air, an anguished appeal to Joseph in her eyes. He got up from his chair at once and went to her. Fran watched them. Joseph taking his wife under her arms and attempting to lift her from her chair. Eleni seemingly struggling against him. Finally, they stood and Fran saw that Joseph was helping Eleni to navigate her way around the furniture towards the door on the far side of the room through which Joseph had entered earlier. As they fought their way across the room Eleni seemed to be striving to tear herself from his grip. She breathed noisily, throttled by phlegm and some asthmatic constriction.

It was a strange, disturbing scene, and so private that Fran felt she should not be a witness to it. These two old people had once been young and beautiful. No remnant of that youth remained to them. Fran could not imagine either of them young. Youth, not death, was that other country which they had left long ago. She was uncomfortable sitting there as their guest by the fire while they fought their way across the room. Were they even going to make it to the door or would they both fall to the floor? She would have to help them up again. The shuffling of their feet and Eleni's loud breathing, each breath ending in a gasp like a bark. Jenny and the cat were not disturbed by it but slept on. Jenny peacefully twitching, her short ears semaphoring her deeper consciousness of events, the cat beyond caring.

Fran was repelled and fascinated. This, she said to herself, as if it were something she had not known before, surprised and appalled by the insight, is the private world of old age. It is the world towards which all our efforts and struggles are leading us. A world of fear and pain and futility, a world of confusion. A place where there is no future left, no hope, but only this certainty of pain and death, and the pain and death of our loved ones. Ever since our childhood we live a lie, for every day of our life, our future stands before us, beckoning us onwards to brighter things, to things that will come to satisfy our hunger for reality. All our life the future is that imagined place into which will be delivered the substance of our dreams. Then comes the truth, this ugly futile beating against exhaustion.

Joseph and Eleni finally made it through the door, which slammed after them as if one of them had fallen back heavily against it, Eleni's voice raised in a lamentation, a howl of frustration and anger. It sent a chill through Fran. She waited, holding her breath in the silence after Eleni's howl. It was so quiet in the apartment now that she could hear the rain. It was coming down heavily, the rolling groans of a distant thunder. Flood rain, her mother would have called this. The creek at the farm would surely be brimming at its banks. She should be at home with Tom and the children. A vast loneliness swept over her at the thought of her family, and the knowledge that she too would soon grow old. To find herself here in this place, on this night, a witness to the ugly end of these people's lives, was terrible.

The fire had burned down. It needed attention. She got up and put another piece of wood on it, then she sat down again and, to distract herself, she opened Valerie Sommers's notebook.

There was a poem. It was titled 'Jessie'.

Am I not her love?
Her valiant saluki?
Her hound of heaven?
My gaze that of a poet dreaming

Of hunting with my mistress.

Jessie is my warrior.
I worship her.
I write my love poetry to her with my eyes.
In their sunlit depths antique visions
Of a buried world are preserved,
For her alone.

Others I examine from a far remove,
My lids half-closed,
Concealing my treasures from their hungry gaze.
As if I were a modest woman,
Displaying only my splendid lashes.
My name is Valerie.
Who is to say I am not worthy of Jessie's love?

The door on the other side of the room opened and Joseph came out. He turned and with great care eased the door closed behind him. He came across to the hearth and picked up a short length of black iron that lay beside the fender and poked at the fire with it. The iron rattled among the burning wood and a crackling flurry of sparks made their frantic escape up the chimney. He reached towards the wood box and selected two of the smaller pieces of split red gum. He placed these on the piece Fran had earlier put on the fire, and he stood and watched till flames began to engulf the pieces of wood, then he turned to Fran.

'Before the pain defeated her, Eleni was a warm and friendly woman. She was tormented by the voices when I met her, but with our love she beat them down and became a happy woman who was known to everyone as a great cook. She was always laughing and making people feel good about themselves. She used to put her hand on people as if she were a priest blessing them and would tell them not to surrender to the despair in their hearts. She relied on her God and He never failed her, except she and I were never blessed with the child she longed for. Now she is angry. Once it was the voices; now pain is her tormentor. In her quiet times she loved to cook and to grow things. She could grow anything. She and Mr Cool understood and loved the earth and the things that grow in it. She would hold a handful of fresh-dug soil under my nose and tell me, Smell that!' He stood looking down at the notebook in Fran's lap, as if he intended to say something about Valerie or her writing. 'Eleni and I never had the child we hoped for. There is nothing left for her.'

Fran was thinking of her university life, the demoralising ethical compromises she was required to make on a daily basis, the endless busyness, the exhausting and pointless distraction of trivia, the loathsomeness of people who had once seemed so nice and caring. She looked up from the notebook and met

Joseph's gaze. 'This is beautiful,' she said. 'Imagine if one could write such things. Have you read it?'

Joseph stood looking down at the fire. 'I came here with my mother in 1950. It must be sixty years ago next May. I was four. We were driven out of the city in a taxi. That taxi ride with my mother is one of my earliest memories. The authorities wanted to put me in an orphanage but my mother made such a fuss they let me come with her. I believe they would have put me in an orphanage after my mother was admitted, but Mrs Cool, the head gardener's wife, was asked to look after me for the day and after that she convinced the department to let her and Mr Cool take care of me. They, too, had no children of their own. I was their child.' He looked doubtfully at Fran. 'Have I told you this already? I remember seeing gum trees for the first time from the taxi.

'Years later, when Sir Arthur decided the grounds of his house needed a new layout, Mr Cool was seconded to the judge's house for the best part of a winter. He took me with him and I got to know that gloomy old house well. I don't think Sir Arthur ever noticed me. He never spoke to me or looked directly at me. I have known no one before or since who could make me feel so convincingly that I had no existence. In Sir Arthur's presence I became a ghost.

'Valerie was eight, I believe, when her mother committed suicide after she became pregnant a second time. After that,

Valerie was alone with her nanny in that vast empty place with its dark wood panelling and enormous reception rooms. She was said to be a troubled child. That was the word they used to describe her: troubled. Who would not be troubled in such a place? She experienced a relapse of her old problem some time after she returned from England—it must have been in 'fifty-six or seven. The judge sent her to see William Vincent-Sinclair, the chief psychiatrist in those days. He was a famous man in the profession. Vincent-Sinclair also had consulting rooms in Collins Street in the city along with all the other great medical men of his day. I don't know what happened to Valerie while she was living with her aunt in England or what she told him about herself, but he must have decided she would benefit from being in a supervised place where he could keep an eye on her. So she was sent here. At first she was given a room downstairs near Sinclair's office and was at liberty to walk in the gardens and to exercise his dog, which she loved to do. By then she was a woman in her thirties. I didn't think she seemed at all mad. She and Jessie Macdonald soon became inseparable and I rarely saw one of them without the other being present. Then, suddenly, they sent Jessie Macdonald away. I believe there was some kind of scandal.

'Like a lot of the patients, Valerie was quiet and lived in her own world without bothering anyone. She would stand there, the dog sitting beside her, and watch me digging and weeding or clipping the hedges. She never spoke but turned away and went on when she was ready. Whenever I caught her eye she smiled, a soft little smile it was, as if she was saying she understood that she and I were just people and it was all one when everything was boiled down. People, and that was that. She and the dog understood each other. She was bereft when it died. It is buried in the chapel grounds. I could see it was in her, this quiet inner knowledge of something. I liked that. It was a mystery and it made me think of the other world of her secret life. And I knew that was something that could never be shared, but must remain hidden and deep and not of this ordinary world. It was Valerie's knowledge of this, I believe, that made her seem mad to ordinary people, who could not understand. No one could tell what she was thinking. They feared that. They resented her mystery. I don't think she was a danger to anyone or to herself. These days I'd say she would not be confined in an asylum. She was thirty-one or thirty-two when she came and she must have been thirty-six when the place was closed down and she was released.'

Joseph was silent, gazing into the fire, thinking back.

Fran said, 'What happened to her?'

Joseph looked at his watch. 'Well, she would have passed away by now, I imagine. I'd better give you a lift to the station. We don't want you to miss this train too.'

'It's all right, Joseph. Thank you, but I have time. I'll walk. I have an umbrella in my office. You can't leave your wife.'

'Eleni has taken her sleeping tablet. She will not wake for a few hours. It will only take me minutes to drive you to the station.'

* * *

Fran didn't ask any more questions of Joseph in the car, but she wanted to know the fate of this woman whose journal had come into her hands in this strange way. It was difficult for her not to feel that the journal had been meant for her. She felt that her possession of it made her responsible to its secrets; responsible to the woman, perhaps, to whom it had once belonged and who had written those words of youthful love. This feeling of being responsible was what her Irish mother said was a *call*. As if something called out to you. Notice me! Don't just walk away. Give me a moment of your attention and I will unfold my meaning to you. A call was also a promise to you of something not yet revealed. It was a word that she, Fran herself, had never used and probably did not believe in. But it came to her mind now all the same, its belief attached to it, seeded there no doubt in her childhood by her mother's belief in the word and in what it stood for—an intuitive need, was it? To give voice to something in order to more fully understand it? To call into being the latent element of desire. This is what she thought.

And so, of course, she thought of *him*. How could she not? Did he *call* to her, yearning for her? Look at the moon!

Joseph parked the car at the entrance to the station. The rain had eased. He said, 'Sir Arthur was in decline by then and I believe Valerie went home to the old place and took care of him. She was there with him till he passed on. After the news of Sir Arthur's death was in the papers I never heard any more of her. I suppose she eventually went into a home or died up there on her own in that gloomy old place.' He sat a moment, then he said, 'It must have been difficult for her to make a good ending of it.'

TWO

On Sunday the weather was fine. A warm winter day after the blessing of the rain. The fields of the farm were bathed in a clear limpid sunlight, the horizon sharp, the air cleansed of dust and smoke. The family was untroubled and content. Tom suggested a picnic. For once, everyone was enthusiastic. When Margie told him their plan, little Tommy emerged from his room straight away, his eyes bleary with the story in his head. He stood in the kitchen watching them, Margie his older sister, his mother and his father, all somehow blending their efforts into a purposeful activity. 'Can I help?' he asked. It was the great question that he will ask for the rest of his life, whenever there is something practical to be done: 'Can

I help?' The mystery of it. And he never will find a helpful way of joining in and his question will rarely be answered. The chores will get done without him, arrangements made, preparations accomplished. The only exception, and the one practical responsibility he will accept as naturally belonging uniquely to himself within this family and to no one else, is setting the fire when it is needed. Little Tommy's fires will always take and burn brightly from the flame of a single match. Fire is something Tommy understands.

On his knees, peering into the open door of the fire box, Tommy is more resolutely solitary even than when he is in his room writing his secret stories, out of sight and out of mind. He kneels before the old iron Ned Kelly wood burner, attending to his ritual, his slight form taking up scarcely any room, selecting his bits and pieces of kindling from his collection, scorning firelighters, closely observing the match flame catch at the shaving of grey boxwood from his father's workshop, feeding in with care the graduated pieces of wood, until he has achieved a blaze and is confident to place large pieces of the split wood into the iron cave of light and heat, at which moment he reluctantly closes the fire door and sits back, watching, the flames dancing in his eyes, observing their magical advance into the substance of the old wood until he feels the iron begin to radiate warmth into the room, and his fire is no longer his own but the property of his family. Then, at last, he gets up and brushes at his knees and steps away, losing interest in his magical creation. Little Tommy, as they called him. He will soon tell his mother that he is not so little these days and maybe they should stop using this diminutive, which he has begun to find irritating.

* * *

They had settled that fine winter Sunday, the four of them, out of the wind, where the stone prow of the ridge broke free from the side of the hill and ended in an abrupt cliff, fifteen metres of golden stone, sunlit and warm, gazing sternly since the beginning of time out over the rich earth of the creek flats. The family sheltered at its base, making their day camp there, away from the chilly breeze that blew steadily across the open country from the far side of the creek. They had boiled the billy and the remnant of Tommy's campfire was still smouldering, a wisp of fragrant smoke rising like a benediction then eddying and breaking in the faint turbulence around the face of the cliff.

Tom, the father, was lying on his back, his head pillowed on a folded towel against the base of the rock, his eyes closed. A large man, at forty-eight Tom Green had begun to lose his youthful conditioning and to soften. He had drunk two cans of beer with his lunch and was drifting pleasantly towards sleep now. The sound of his daughter's voice on her mobile, speaking to one of her new schoolfriends, and the fresh in the creek tumbling over the stones, the beer, and the warm sun on his face inducing in him the feeling that his problems were sure to resolve themselves. Tom was most at peace in the company of his family. Well fed, warmed by the winter sun, reassured by the sound of his daughter's voice and the pleasant drift of alcohol in his brain, secure in the love of his wife, Tom had begun to dream.

Fran was sitting on the spread blanket two metres from her husband, the remains of their meal around her. The air fragrant with the damp smell of the soil and the crushed stems of the grass. Margie's voice came to her, the girl's sudden bursts of laughter, her delight and anxiety in her new friendships. Watching her daughter walking about on the flats, Fran saw that she had become a woman and was a child no longer. She was striding around, back and forth, measuring a circle of ground with her fierce steps, drawing further and further away from them, looking down and listening intently, serious one moment, then looking up and laughing. But where was Tommy? The fourth of them? Fran looked around but couldn't see him. Their reliable maker of fire whenever it was needed. The mysterious one among them. Had anyone noticed what direction he had taken when he wandered off?

Fran drank the last of the wine in her glass and stood up. She leaned down and picked up her towel and Valerie Sommers's journal and, with a glance at her sleeping husband, she stepped away from the camp and walked out onto the flats. She had not had a moment alone without the demands of work since Joseph had given her the little book and she was eager to discover more of Valerie's private world of dreams and poetry, the agonies and the delights of the troubled young woman on whom she was ready to bestow an imaginary life. There was a comfort for her in feeling the little book in her hand as she walked across the flats away from Tom and her daughter, towards the bank of the creek. There was no sign of Tommy. The bank of the creek was steep and thickly overgrown with willows and blackberries, the far bank in deep shadow, the sun already well down towards the western horizon. The previous year, their first on the farm, they had cleared a path down the bank to the stream. Here the creek opened into a deep hole, where in summer they swam, before the stream tumbled in a flurry of agitation over a lip of rock, carrying on noisily along a stretch of shallows, where floods had cut deep through the ancient silt deposits to the old stones of an earlier creek bed.

Fran set her towel on the grass and placed Valerie's notebook on top of it. She took off her sandals and pulled up her skirt and sat on the towel with her bare legs in the water. She drew in her breath sharply at the chill of the water against her skin. Soon after they bought the place and came to live here, their neighbour, Ina Turner, paid them a visit one Sunday afternoon. She presented them with a welcoming bottle of her preserved pears and sat in the kitchen with them and told them stories of the area. She had lived alone with her dog and her goats on the ridge, she said, since the death of her husband Jim seven years earlier. The creek, she revealed, was fed by springs that had their source deep within the earth, under the ancient volcanoes that dotted the landscape. In more than seventy years she had never seen the creek run dry, even at the end of the hottest summer and through the longest drought. Ina had spoken of the sources of the clear water as if the knowledge was something she had dreamed. Since then, Fran could not think of the creek without seeing the dreamlike images of the deep sub-volcanic places of its origins.

As she sat there now, her buttocks resting on her towel, the shock of the cold water on her legs making her close her eyes and take a deep breath, Fran was seeing Ina's mystical dreamlike spirits of the ancient volcanic springs which gave life to the land. This knowledge that the water came from deep within the earth, emerging from an ancient source in the dark of evolutionary time, had lent to the water of the creek a quality of magical purity. There had been sleepless nights when she had got up, put on her dressing-gown and left the house. She had walked down to the creek and stood on the bank above the swimming hole and looked at a great white moon reflected in the tranquil pool, and she had felt herself to be in

touch with something beautiful and real and timeless, something that could never be touched by the dismal pretensions of
the university life, something in which even her own childhood
dreams were resurrected.

Fran saw in Ina a fearless woman, weathered and independent, living up there on the stony ridge in her cottage with her
mild-eyed dog and her goats and her few acres. A woman from
another time. A solitary survivor from the past, knowing the old
claims on the land, familiar with the daily handwork of her life,
her steel tools as sharp as razors, their wooden handles of her
own fashioning. Sitting on the bank of the creek now, Valerie's
little book beside her, Fran was comforted by the regular thump
of Ina's axe from the ridge. It was a companionable sound.
A reassurance for her that something so essentially good could
survive here.

Among the tangle of willows on the far bank small birds
flitted about busily. Fran didn't know what sort of birds they
were; finches, perhaps, or maybe silvereyes. She watched them
for a while then picked up the journal and opened it.

The entry didn't have a heading. It was dated 18 July 1960,
winter, so it must have been Valerie's third year in the mental
hospital. As she read, Fran was seeing Valerie sitting on a
narrow single bed against the wall where her own desk now

stood, the barred window in darkness, the heavy door closed against a hostile world.

It is late. I am cold. My watch has stopped. I forgot to wind it earlier, but it must be after midnight. I have decided to kill myself. Sister Marion came to see me this afternoon. I have known Sister Marion as a deeply Christian woman. She has always been kind to me and has helped me in many ways from the day of my arrival in this place. She is unwell now with some undiagnosed problem that weakens her. Perhaps it is her heart. She does not complain. Earlier this evening she sat beside me on my bed here and took my hands in both her own hands and struggled to meet my gaze for the emotion that was in her.

My dread was great. I said, 'What is it, Sister Marion?' I knew she must have some news for me. My heart scarcely had the courage to continue beating while I waited to hear what she would say. I feared to hear this news, for I knew already what it must be. I did not wish to have my fear confirmed but wanted to go on nurturing the faint glimmer of hope that was left to me. I knew that in a moment Sister Marion was going to extinguish that hope forever. The truth horrified me, but I would not delay it. I looked at her and she closed her eyes and gathered her resolve, then she opened her eyes and looked directly into my eyes, confronting the difficulty of her task with her usual courage, and for an infinite moment she did not speak. Then the words of my fate came out of her mouth and nothing ever again will be restored to me: 'Dr Sinclair received a telephone call from the director of Aradale hospital this morning,' she said, and was overcome once again at this point and could not continue. Outwardly I was calm and I put my arm around her shoulders and said to her, 'It is all right, Sister Marion. You mean to help me. This is difficult for you and I am sorry.' She looked at me with gratitude and lowered her head and murmured, 'Your Jessie has hung herself.' At this she choked on her emotion and wept helplessly into her hands.

Despite my most earnest resolve I was unable to speak for a good minute or two. At last I found my voice and spoke her name, just once. *Jessie*, I said, my voice no longer my own but that of a broken stranger. I knew I would follow her into death. It was a deep, secret relief to know it. I did not weep or cry out, but sat quietly on my bed beside Sister Marion—her distress was great and I did my best to comfort her. There was within me a beautiful strange calm place from where I coolly contemplated the release from suffering that I shall find in that place beyond grief. Death offers me my release. I gladly accept it. I am broken but they will not defeat us, nor shall we be their victims any longer. They shall never again defile the purity of our love with the evil of their prohibitions.

Sister Marion said a prayer, and she kissed the crucifix which she wears around her neck, then she held it out for me to kiss. I took it in my hand and gazed at it. It was not new to me. I had known it at school. Every classroom possessed one. Every hallway and office and dormitory had its crucifix in plain sight. Now I saw it as a thing stripped of its authority and its mystique, a malevolent, evil thing.

Sister Marion said, 'Take comfort in our Lord Jesus, Valerie. He is our Saviour and our haven.'

I said to her, without anger or rancour in my voice, but with the clear conviction of someone who has chosen the moment of their own death, 'I cannot take comfort in a creed that celebrates the image of a man being tortured to death.' I handed the thing back to her and she took it from me and let it swing against her breasts.

'Oh, Valerie,' she said. 'That is hard.'

Hard? Was it hard? I asked myself. And I was compelled to remind her then of what she already knew of me. 'When I was found to be sleeping together with my friend at school they expelled me, but not before cruelly humiliating us in the name of that tormented image of yours. My father sent me to live with my aunt in

England to avoid the scandal of it. And when I and my
darling Jessie were found together here last year and it was
plain to the director and to the matron that Jessie and I
were lovers—for we made no secret of it but were proud
to show our love before the gaze of the world—we were
humiliated and punished in the name of the proprieties of
your creed. You separated us. You condemned us. Now you
come to tell me my Jessie has despaired in that hellhole of
Aradale where you sent her and has hung herself. And you
offer to comfort me with that thing you wear around your
neck. You ask me to kiss your effigy of a tormented man.
Where is the love you speak of in any of this? There are
no flowers, there is no poetry in your creed, no sunlight or
hope or the celebration of human life in it. Sister Marion,
I have been tormented enough.'

I stood up. I pitied her and did not pity myself.
I had already known the news she brought me before
she delivered it. For Jessie would have said my name.
My name would have been the last word my darling
Jessie spoke before she took the fatal step and ended her
life. I can hear her voice speaking my name for the last
time—*Valerie*—and in her last enunciation of my name
she would have accumulated all our hopes, all our love, all
our anguish and all our despair. She would not have wept,

just as I have not wept, not yet, though I know I surely
shall. My heart heard my name called by her before ever
the director knew of her death. *I* knew it! They did not
know it. Now I am alone with her. They cannot make us
suffer anymore. We shall not be parted. We have liberated
ourselves from their cruelty. They frown and speak of love,
and they caress us even as they deliver their cruel words
which condemn us. No, I do not despair. I reject despair
and I rejoice. Our love lives within us.

I stood beside my bed, waiting for Sister Marion to
recover her composure. It was difficult for her to get
up again once she had sat down, and my bedsprings
are inclined to sag. I said softly, 'Your Jesus cult knows
nothing of love but only of cruelty. Where is that love, the
forgiveness you speak of? Where is it? You condemned us
without pity. Your cruelty has no end and no forgiveness in
it. Your faith is pitiless. Your god is nothing but a tyrant.'

She was struggling. I took her arm and helped her to
stand and she looked at me with great sorrow in her gaze.
She is, after all, a sad and gentle woman, her innocent self
beguiled and lost and ever alone with her doubt.

A sound behind her made Fran start. She turned around.
Tommy was coming down the bank towards her. She closed

the journal. 'Hi, darling!' She held out her hand to him and he took it and came alongside her and sat down on the grass.

'Aren't your legs cold?' he said.

Fran laughed. 'Freezing.' She lifted her legs out of the water and leaned down and rubbed at her shins. Her ankles were numb.

'They've gone red,' he said.

'They'll warm up. And what have you been doing?' She wanted to hug him but she noticed he was subdued and inwards with his own thoughts. He was such a solitary little boy. He had made one friend at school who had come out to the farm once for a sleepover and had not come again. She was feeling the presence of Valerie, her words sharing her own deepest knowledge of suffering and bliss and the mystery of herself. She was feeling trusted and intimate with the words of the young writer, the woman alone in what was now her own office. Reaching for this deeper contact with her own interior life, it required a conscious effort from her to reach out to her son.

'I've been watching the white rabbit,' he said. Tommy was tearing at a clod of grass and earth from the bank with something he was holding in his hand. When he had liberated the clod of matted grass roots from the grip of the earth, he threw it into the pool with a sudden violent movement that startled Fran. 'It's not scared of me,' he said. 'The brown ones run back into the blackberries when they see me coming but the white one sits up on his hind legs and looks at me.' He began digging again with the thing in his hand. 'He signals to me with his ears.'

Fran reluctantly set Valerie's notebook aside on her towel. 'Who signals to you?'

Tommy looked at her. In his eyes was hurt and accusation. 'My friend, the white rabbit. I sat down and we looked at each other for a long time. I signalled back to him by wagging my head. He wants to get to know me better.'

'That's wonderful, darling.'

He ripped out another clod of earth and tossed it into the pool. 'What happened in China?'

A stab of adrenaline thrust at her heart, sharp and immediate. She flinched and let out a small tight murmur of dismay. She had no idea how to respond. A brown stain was spreading slowly in the pure clarity of the water where the clod of earth had fallen, the grass floating, drowning, bleeding its awful brown stain into the pure spring water that had risen from its sacred source deep in the mysterious ground of the volcanoes. The sight of the spreading stain disheartened Fran. She put her hand on Tommy's arm. 'Oh, don't throw any more, please!' she begged him. She saw that the thing in his hand was a knife.

He was working at freeing a new clod with the blade. 'I heard Margie and Dad talking about it.'

She waited. They couldn't possibly know. Unless someone had said something to Tom at the pub. Some random connection, his wife and the Chinese scholar in the photograph. But what? She looked at her son. 'What did they say?'

'Margie asked Dad why things were different between you two since you got back.'

'And do you think things are different?'

He shrugged. He was frowning at the knife, on which he had speared the mixture of earth and grass. 'Can I throw it?'

'If you must,' she said. 'Where did you get that knife?' She was so close to despair; the beautiful day of the picnic and Valerie's journal had turned black and threatening.

Tommy stood up and hurled the clod forcefully straight down into the pool close to the bank.

Fran yelped and pulled her feet away from the edge. 'Tommy! You nearly hit me with it! You've splashed me with the mud!'

He stood looking into the water, the steel blade hanging from his fingers. 'The white rabbit is curious about me.'

'You could say you're sorry.'

'Sorry,' he murmured unhappily, reluctant, saddened by life, by whatever it was that had changed the tone of his life, something he understood but did not understand, gnawing at him to set it right, to erase it, to prove it was not true, to return everything to the way it had been before his mother went to China. He wiped the mud from the blade by sliding two fingers along it. 'Ina gave it to me.' He held the blade out in front of him, not exactly brandishing it, but admiring it, turning it this way then that so that the sun glanced off it and made him squint.

'I don't like it,' she said. 'Can you please put it down?'

A splodge of wet mud had landed on the notebook. Fran stood up and wiped the mud from the cover with the hem of her skirt. A stain remained on the cover. She looked at Tommy, standing nervously beside her now. She was afraid he would run back up the bank and go off in search of his new friend, the white rabbit. 'And what did your father say?'

'Dad said don't worry about it. He said nothing's really changed.'

'And what do you think? Do you think anything changed? Aren't we all just the same? We all love each other just the same, don't we?'

He said sullenly, with conviction, 'It's not the same.' He looked at her.

She said, 'Let me give you a cuddle. For God's sake, put that knife down. Whatever made Ina give it to you?'

'It was Jim's. It was given to him in Canada when he was a boy. She said Jim would have given it to me if he'd still been alive. She said I must keep it until I am old, then I must give it to my son, or to a special young friend.' He held it out flat on his palm. 'It's heavier than it looks.' He gazed at the knife balanced on his hand. 'Dad said I'm lucky to have a friend like Ina.'

'Your father said that? He knows about the knife?'

'She says Dad's a real neighbour.' He clasped the bone handle of the knife and put it behind his back and looked squarely at Fran. 'I'm going to live in her house after she's dead.'

Fran was shocked. 'Oh, darling. You mustn't say that. Ina isn't going to die for a long, long time yet.'

'We all die,' he said, matter-of-fact, and he looked off across the waterhole. 'She admires Dad. She's got an illness. She's not going to last forever. No one lasts forever. We all die.' He turned to her.

She said, 'Tommy!' She took him in her arms and held him firmly against her. 'I love you!'

He stood against her, not resisting but not responding, his arms slack at his sides, the bone handle of the knife in his right hand.

She kissed the top of his head. 'Oh, Tommy! Tommy!'

'I'm not little anymore.'

'I didn't call you little.'

His voice was a murmur, muffled by her breasts pressing against him, the soft material of her blouse, the smell of mother in his nostrils. 'I love you, Mum.'

'I know you do, darling.'

He put his arms around her and hugged her. 'It's all right, Mum. Don't cry.'

'If anything happened to any of you, I'd just die. I wouldn't go on.'

'Mum! Nothing's going to happen to us. Don't say that! You're scaring me!' He pulled away from her and looked up into her eyes. 'Don't cry! I'll give Ina the knife back if you really hate it.'

'I'm sorry, I'm not crying.' She got out her handkerchief and wiped her eyes and blew her nose. 'There! It's all right. Keep Jim's knife. Ina's right.'

'Were the Chinese mean to you? Is that what it was?'

'God, no! What a thing to say. No, they were lovely. Everyone was friendly and respectful.'

He stood looking at her. 'But what?'

'But nothing! Really. Nothing.'

'Dad told Margie things always change when one person goes away for a while.'

'I was only away for seventeen days.'

He was ten and here was his mother lying to him, and he knew his mother was lying to him, and he didn't know how to sort things out with her. It was no good her excusing herself by saying children don't understand. Children do understand. Children sense things at once. They understand everything. Children understand the truth more clearly than grown-ups. They have highly tuned antennae and register the smallest changes in the mood of the family. Their thoughts are not cluttered with ambitions. Children fear the death of their parents. They may not know exactly what's going on, but they know something is going on. I am lying to my son, she confessed to herself sorrowfully, when I tell him nothing happened in China. She closed her eyes. What could she do? Tommy was like a stranger. She ached with love for him. She wanted to save him.

'Dad said it's normal. He said we all change all the time but don't notice it till someone goes away then comes back after a while.'

'Did he say that? And what did Margie say?'

'She said, That's bullshit and you know it.'

'Margie!'

'Do you think it's bullshit, Mum?'

'No. Your father's probably right. Things do change. We all change. I'm three different people most days. But I hate it. I wish things didn't change. I wish we could all go on being the same, just being us, our family.' She saw that he was gazing devotedly at the knife again, holding the blade out and sliding a finger along the flat of it. Everything had changed. Everything. She was dismayed. She could see no way back to her innocence.

They stood side by side at the edge of the pool, a deep silence between them. She looking at the water, he looking at the knife. Was he waiting for the truth to come out of his mother's mouth? The sun had gone down below the western hills. The pool was dark and cold and forbidding. The birds in the willows had fallen silent. Fran looked down at her son and met his expectant gaze. 'Shall we go and see if the white rabbit has waited for you?'

'It will have gone home by now.' He took her hand. 'Dad fixed Ina's tank stand for her. It was rotting and leaning over to one side. He had to buy an electric drill. He bought it specially for Ina. For the old red gum. He said it would have taken him away from his own work for a week without an electric drill. I told him Ina's husband didn't have any electric tools and was never in a hurry to get things done so long as he did them the right way. I told him to take the drill back. Ina said we should never be in a hurry if we want to live properly.'

'And is your father going to take the drill back?'

'He's keeping it now. I was in Ina's orchard with her and we could hear the drill going and she said she hated that sound more than anything. She does everything the way Jim did things. Properly. I will be like that when she's dead and I live up there on my own. I'll have my own dog and some goats too.'

They walked up the slope from the flats towards the cottage.

Tommy said, 'She made Dad promise to bury her in her orchard after she dies. He promised her he would do that, but then he told me afterwards he was just being nice to her saying that, and we're not allowed to bury people just anywhere where they want to be buried. I think it would be good if I live there to know Ina was in the orchard.'

'I thought you wanted to write your stories when you're grown up?'

'I wrote the story of Jim getting the knife when he was a boy and gave it to Ina. I drew a picture of the knife. I called it "Jim's Knife". I can write in her place after she's dead and still have a dog and some goats.'

The air was cold as they neared the cottage. Fran said, 'Will you light the wood fire?'

'No worries, Mum. Are you feeling better now?'

'Yes, darling. Of course. Don't worry about me.'

'Ina said you're an accomplished city woman.'

'Is that what she said? Accomplished? Goodness.'

'She told Dad that.'

'And what did he say?'

'He just laughed.'

'And what do you think?'

'Ina's right, Mum. We're all proud of you.'

'Thank you, darling.'

They went into the kitchen. The flywire door banged behind them. Tom had left the rug and the picnic things on the floor. The empty wine bottle lay on its side. Margie was in her room talking on her phone. Fran supposed Tom must have gone over to his workshop. She put her towel and Valerie's notebook on the kitchen table then she filled the kettle and set it on the gas. She put leaves in the pot and stood waiting for the water to boil. Tommy was crouched in front of the wood stove, peering in at the beginnings of his fire. The knife lay on the rug beside him. Fran stood by the kettle, waiting, her eyes closed. She felt deeply tired. There was a buzzing in her ears.

F ran was about to walk down to Sunbury station to catch her
usual train home. She was in good time and was standing in
her office with her overcoat on and her satchel over her shoulder,
ready to go. She took one final look around, checking that she
wasn't forgetting something. Her phone rang. She put the satchel
down and pulled the phone out of the bag. Carlos Skänder,
the Dean of Studies, wanted to change the time of the scheduled meeting in the morning. He was in one of his blustering,
bullying moods. She knew at once what the real story would
be. Something more interesting to him than the meeting had
come up and he was changing things around at the last minute
to suit his own selfish agenda. She had been organised and on

time. Now this! So far as Skänder was concerned they could all rearrange their diaries for the morning just to suit him. Well, to hell with him, she thought. She decided to confront him. She did her best to butt in but he rushed on, getting louder and more threatening and talking over the top of her and refusing to give way to her voice. He had decided he was going to insist and her voice, in the end, wasn't strong enough to overpower his. She was beaten back by him. It was his guilt that made him bully her. She knew this. She wanted to scream. But she didn't scream. Instead of screaming at him, her resolve began to wilt in the face of his insane barrage. All right! All right! For God's sake, calm down! You'll give yourself a fucking heart attack, you old shit! If only! It was her mother who used to say only the good die young. Skänder would live to be a hundred at that rate.

It wasn't only the time of the meeting he wanted her to change, but the participants and the items on the agenda. In the end he changed everything. Her own original agenda, which she had put a lot of thought into and which was the result of careful consultation with her staff, had enjoyed his approval. Now it was tossed out and replaced by his weird ad-hoc collection of items that no one else would be briefed on. And why did he want that creepy sleaze Eric Thornton to sit in on the meeting with them?

She took off her overcoat and hung it back on its hanger. She felt inadequate, frustrated, tired and defeated. It angered and saddened her that she couldn't face down Skänder. She stood a moment, recovering her balance, being real about it, being professional. Valerie was not with her in the cell tonight. The ghost had left. Her cell was vacant, cold, empty.

She sat at her desk, opened her laptop again and composed a memo with the new meeting time and agenda and emailed it to the new list of attendees, marking it urgent. Before she could close her computer, two of the recipients wrote back sharp little messages to say they couldn't make the new time and asking why she had changed the agenda at the last minute. The second of these emails upset her. It was from Claire Pollard, a woman she liked and had supported in her appeal against a charge of inappropriate behaviour by one of the second-year students. Claire's email said: *This is so typical of your leadership style, Fran. It really is completely thoughtless and uncaring of you.* She found this depressing. She expected a certain amount of bullying and pressure from above, but she'd never expected her colleagues to attack her in this way, especially someone she'd gone out of her way to support. She remembered now the cautionary words of Stella Colvin, the psychologist who'd briefed her when she was appointed head of school. Stella warned her, 'You're going to learn things about people you'll wish you never knew.' She'd let Stella's warning go in one ear and out the other. Back then she'd been fired up with ambition, focused on taking the next step towards the professorship that was to give point and meaning to her life. She was not then the person she had since become.

* * *

On the train at last, she took Valerie's journal from her bag and turned to the end of the section about Jessie's suicide. Two blank pages came after it. There were inky fingerprints and a few indecipherable smudges and stains on these pages but no legible writing. A word scribbled in one corner, crossed out then repeated. But she couldn't make it out. The neatly ordered lines of carefully composed prose ended with the description of Sister Marion as a gentle woman. Fran turned the pages. There were several blanks. The next formal entry was dated 12 February 1961. Seven months after Valerie's confident assurance to the diary that she was going to end her own life! Fran felt enormous relief to see this. That wound had healed sufficiently for her to live with it.

> It is late afternoon. A warm day. I am sitting on the
> bench here in the director's garden, watching the rainbow
> lorikeets eating the ripe apples on the old apple tree that
> I fell in love with the day I arrived here. The apple tree
> reminds me of who I was then. The tree is hollow now
> and a great limb has broken from it. When Mr Cool came

to clear away the debris of the broken limb he told me
he too loved the apple tree. Mr Cool came to Australia
from Scotland when he was a young man and still has
their lovely way of speaking, as if the music of their words
is still with them. I asked him if he knew what sort of
apples they were. He said the tree was a Cox's Orange
Pippin. What a lovely name! I have not forgotten it. Mr
Cool and his boy, Joseph, those two share a private world
of gardeners' dreams. Watching them at work calms me.
Gardening is a kind of meditation with them. They seem
to know the truth of things and their inner simplicity.
I have never seen either of them hurry. It is as if for them
life will go on forever and there will always be time to
push the wheelbarrow along the path down past the Scots
pines and empty the contents of it with a fork onto the
mulch pile that steams on cold mornings and sends a smell
of decay over the grounds when the breeze is from the
west. And there will be time for Mr Cool to charge his
pipe and light it and stand a moment while the fragrance
of his tobacco blends with the smell of the pine trees. Time
is of no consequence to those two. For Mr Cool and Joseph
time does not pass but just exists. I longed to touch the
magic of their lives and one day I put my hand on Joseph's
shoulder. It felt natural for me to do this. When my hand
rested on his shoulder he paused in his work and looked

at me, and I saw in his beautiful eyes an understanding deeper than my own.

Almost half the tree is gone. The rest of this wounded tree will fall one day soon. I hope it does not fall before I fall. When I spoke to Mr Cool of my fear that the apple tree would fall altogether, he replied to me in the tones of a man who is amused by life. He set to one side the hoe he was working with and attended to his pipe, which had gone out. After he had taken a couple of trial puffs, he took the pipe from between his lips and examined it, tamping it with his thumb. His thumb is dark brown, deeply stained and burned by the hot tobacco. Then he looked at me and said, 'That old tree will outlive us both.' And he reached for the hoe and resumed chipping between the rows of cabbages.

The gaudy rainbow lorikeets have come in their pairs and trustingly feed on the apples. They hang upside down for preference and converse quietly with their partner, sharing their delight in the tasty apples that are really quite overripe. Many windfalls lie at the base of the tree. The director's dog, Sally, watches the lorikeets sleepily from beside my feet. The lorikeets ignore our presence. There are no white cockatoos today to frighten these small birds. The early evening air is lovely and warm.

In this quiet garden I wait for the end of another summer.

* * *

Fran stood alone in the car park at Castlemaine Railway Station, looking up at the sky. She had dreamed of her Mongol warrior last night, a dream so vivid and so real that the smell of his body was in her nostrils when she woke. Her whole day had been haunted by the afterglow of the dream, that delicious torment she had come to know. But she had not had a moment during the day to dwell on it. The dream terrified her, it thrilled her, and it made her guilty. So there! She did feel guilty after all! The dream had been like a message from another world. Her own inner world, so far away from her email realities she could not coerce its presence but must wait for something else to bring it close. It was at times almost as if she had made it up. That world. That night in Hefei. It was a world over which she had no conscious control but which she longed for with a kind of madness that was denied by the so-called sane world of never-ending trivia in which she spent her working days. Valerie's diary was her consolation. She kept it by her. It was her assurance of something finer. Her fingers touched it and she felt grateful to be its keeper. Valerie's diary belonged to the same world as her night in Hefei.

The stars were so bright after the rain they really did shimmer, quite as if the universe was trembling with some apocalyptic preparation. In a moment, surely, the old gods would awaken and announce their final decision. There would be a blinding flash and the human experiment would be over. Not with a bang or a whimper, just over, done, finished as if it had never been. There would be no word for it. No poetry. Humanity would have failed to invent the word for its own end. Only the old gods would be left to appreciate this irony, if that is what it was. There would no longer be a use for words, neither new ones nor the old ones. Just the shimmering silence of the eternal sky, the womb of expectation, to be loved without words, to *make* love without words, the dream of the gods we have spurned. She stood there, the solitary figure of a woman standing in the empty car park gazing up at the brilliant night sky over country Victoria after rain. And there was the smell of the forest in the air.

There was only one other vehicle in the car park. A black ute. It was parked under the light beside her Renault, which seemed a bit odd with the rest of the large car park empty. There would be a hard frost by morning. Fran loved standing there alone in the cold night looking up at the sky, at the edge of the universe, looking out into infinity. The ache in her belly had been there all day. It was not hunger for food. The impossibility of ever seeing him again and knowing that world with him flooded her being with the delicious melancholy of the vast night sky. Everything real was impossible. There was so much beauty in the world it made her despair to think of it. Why was there never any time for the wonderful things that mattered to her? This life she had created! It came back to her that Tommy had asked her, Were the Chinese mean to you? She wondered now, with a pang of guilt, if Tommy was being picked on at school. She felt a surge of protective pity for him, a longing for some kind of perfect union of understanding with her son, an understanding in which lies could never find a place and he would be protected from all suffering and unpleasantness. He was so grown up already with his knife, so innocent in his certainties. That his suffering had not occurred to her when he asked her that question shamed her now. 'I'm so incredibly selfish,' she said aloud. She would ask him in the morning if any of the boys at school ever bullied him. The idea of it was a torment.

She got out her phone and called Tom. 'I'm just at the car now.'

He said, 'You must be starving. I'll heat up some soup. It's freezing here.'

'Thanks. How was Tommy after school? He's not being picked on, is he?'

'Tommy was fine. I really don't think you need worry about him. He's not the great football hero, but I have a feeling he knows how to take care of himself. He's small and intense and a bit weird, but he's not a vulnerable kind of boy. They're the ones who get bullied, the vulnerable ones. Tommy will look them in the eye and they'll know it will cost them to have a go at him. That's the way it works.'

It seemed to Fran quite often that she and Tom saw a different person in Tommy. She was tired and didn't want to get involved in some kind of discussion in which she knew their attitudes would never quite meet up.

He said, 'I'll see you when you get home. Drive carefully. And watch out for the kangas! They'll be on the move. We've had a heap of rain. It bucketed down for an hour before it cleared up earlier.'

She hung up and unlocked the car. A figure was sleeping in the ute parked next to the Renault. Sleeping or dead? She drove out of the car park and turned onto the road towards home. In the rear-view mirror she saw the black ute pull out onto the road and turn in the opposite direction. She was glad it wasn't following her.

Her headlights danced on the narrow strip of the black road ahead of her. She was seeing Valerie sitting by the apple tree that late summer afternoon, the dog at her feet and the lorikeets in the wounded tree. Stealing time to read Valerie's journal on the train had steadied her after the crackpot day. Skänder and the awfulness of his voice rising against her like a wave coming in, swamping her, then that final bitter word of Claire Pollard's miserable message. Valerie's had surely been a life of real suffering. But hadn't it also been a life of great beauty?

Hadn't Valerie's life shared the unutterable beauty that Fran herself had struggled to know, that sweet strangeness, whenever she allowed herself to think of her moment in the hotel room in that faraway imaginary city of Hefei? It was like a memory of a storybook from childhood. A castle on a hill with a maiden alone in a room, inaccessible at the top of the tower. Another life. China, a place of mystery and promise.

She wanted a definite connection between herself and Valerie. She knew, her instincts knew it, that such a link existed if only it could find its way through her tumult to an expression of itself. She needed time to think. Time to reflect. There was never any time. Then the simplicity of it would unfold. Valerie's poetry would become her own moment in a landscape of real reality. She said aloud, 'In that other life in that other world.' She knew what she meant. Claire Pollard's bitterness hurt. In that job, no one had ever thanked her. Not once. She closed her eyes for a second then opened them.

The road was narrow with great old gum trees lining the verges. Through the meaningless chaos of her day, she desperately wanted to rescue her belief that Valerie Sommers would have understood her in a way no one else would ever understand her. Surely Valerie would not speak of her understanding, but would smile, that same gentle smile of knowing as when she rested her hand on Joseph's shoulder. That! She loved that. If only she could express the mystery of it the way Valerie expressed it.

She cried out and stamped on the brake pedal, her heart pounding. The Renault skidded into the corner and came to a jolting stop, its front wheels off the gravel, dug into the grass verge, the headlights picking up the silent forms of cattle out in the paddock beyond the shelter of trees, the great beasts gazing silently. She sat and waited, her heart thudding in her chest. Something had been sitting silently in her head for a long time, ignored and unattended to. The dark old portrait of the woman hanging on the wall behind the dean's desk in his office. It must surely be a likeness of Valerie? When Carlos Skänder was leading the group of VIPs around on the opening day, she remembered him proudly showing them his office. He had them all in there, lined up and looking at what he said was the work of a famous portraitist. A famous Australian artist, he said. She didn't register the name. A woman. The picture was one of the treasures in the university's art collection. A portrait of the daughter of Sir Arthur Sommers, once the Chief Justice of the High Court of Australia and a friend of the director of the mental hospital. The dean was inventing the pedigree of the place for them. Not just a nut house, but a centre of culture, if you believed him. This artist had been commissioned to paint a portrait of the judge and had then painted the judge's daughter.

The car had stalled. She was sitting there, the headlights piercing the trees, touching the solid forms of the silent beasts out there in the paddock. Fran had often been in the dean's office but had never taken any particular notice of the painting on the wall behind his desk. She'd had an impression that day of an unsmiling young woman with short hair, her gaze directed off to one side. A brown, rather dull picture, she had thought it. The poet, the vice-chancellor had called the young woman. She would go into the dean's office in the morning and have a look. Skänder wouldn't be in until the meeting at the stupid new time of just after lunch. What an idiot the man was!

She started the engine, backed off the verge and drove onto the narrow gravel road. It wasn't kangaroos but Valerie she'd had to watch out for.

She opened the back door and went in. She stood, absorbing the warmth and stillness of the house. The familiar smell of Tom's reliable leek and potato soup in the kitchen. From where she was standing she could see him. He was sitting on the couch in front of the wood stove in the living room. He was asleep, his head fallen back, his mouth open. He was developing a small paunch. A bottle of their Blackjack shiraz was on the table, an empty wineglass beside it. She supposed both children were in their beds. A night-bird repeatedly called the single note nature had given to it. She went into the living room and stood in front of Tom and looked down at him. He had been reading last weekend's copy of *The Age*. The pages of the newspaper were scattered on the floor at his feet. His feet were encased in the weird knitted raw wool socks with leather soles that he'd bought at the pharmacy. They were bunched at his ankles like ballet dancers' leg warmers. Margie had teased him about them. Fran turned away and was about to tiptoe to the bedroom and get changed when Tom opened his eyes and sat up.

'I didn't want to wake you.'

He rubbed his face with his hands and got up. 'You were quick.'

'You've been asleep.'

'I'll heat the soup.' He paused on his way to the kitchen and turned back to her. 'Are you okay?'

'I'm exhausted.' She spoke calmly, and might have been saying, I like your socks. He was waiting to hear more. 'It's been another one of those days. That's all. I won't bore you. Go and get the soup. I'll get out of these things.'

He stood, considering her.

'What?' she said.

'I wonder,' he said, 'if you're ever going to tell me you've had a satisfying day in that job of yours?'

'Probably not.'

'You used to. You used to love it. Remember?'

No, she didn't remember. She refused to remember. She went on and opened the bedroom door and went in and closed it behind her. She had been naive then. Why did her home sometimes demand from her the last vestiges of her patience for the day? She had nothing more to call on. Nothing more to give. She sat on the bed. There was a persistent high-pitched whistling somewhere. She wiggled her finger in the left ear then the right. The tuneless whistling went up a half-tone. She was sure she was forgetting something important but knew she wasn't going to be able to think of what it was. Her brain had decided to shut down. Whoever was in charge had closed the gate and run away. You couldn't blame them.

* * *

They sat side by side on the couch, their steaming soup in the Chinese bowls on their knees. She reached for her glass and took a drink of the dark ruby wine. The room was cosy and warm, the wood heater glowing. She was wearing her green dressing-gown. The rich soft green of the gown made her hair look darker and glossier. She felt comfortable wearing it. At home. Safe. The gown's familiar soft embrace made her feel more herself than anything else she had ever owned. She had worn it to the hospital with Tommy. It was new for that occasion then, the second baby. The nurses had admired it. It still looked fresh even now. She would never part with it. She would never find another one like it.

Tom said, 'Are you still reading that diary or whatever it was?'

She went on spooning the soup, enjoying being in her dressing-gown sitting in front of the fire. She wanted to ask him to please not speak but for once to just let things drift down there in the silence. Did Tom have a silence in him? She had never been sure. That was the trouble. She knew that. He was not like his son, little Tommy. Tom was quiet, but he did not commune with his own inner silence the way little Tommy did. There was a difference. She suspected that Tommy had an immense silence. It frightened her to think of it. Like a distant horizon in him. She and little Tommy were more alike. That frightened her too. The night-bird was still sounding its solitary note.

Tom said, 'Don't you feel as if you're prying into that woman's private life? I don't think I could bear to read someone's old diary. Especially someone you never knew.'

'I'd quite like another glass of wine, but that bottle seems to be empty.'

'Sorry. Yes. I should have waited. But I needed a drink. It hasn't been the most productive day I've ever had either. Shall I open another Blackjack? We've only got four left.'

'Open one!'

He got up and went out to the kitchen. She heard him clinking bottles. He came back into the room and stood by the table pouring wine into her glass. 'When did she die?'

'Who?'

Tom filled his own glass. 'The woman of the diary.'

'I don't know.'

'Is she nineteenth century?'

She leaned and placed her empty bowl on the table and tucked her legs under her, gathering the generous folds of her robe and wrapping the soft material around her knees. She bent forward to pick up the glass of wine and held it in both hands. She didn't take a drink but sat staring at the window of the fire. The bird outside in the night repeating its single cry. There was something deeply companionable about its presence out there, persisting the way it did.

Tom said in a slightly piqued voice, 'So you're not going to ask me about my day, then?'

'Sorry! How was your day, darling?'

'The bitch cancelled her order for the dining setting.'

'Oh no! You're joking! Fuck her! What made her do that? *Can* she do that?'

'She did it.' He was silent.

She looked at him. 'What?'

He reached for his glass and drained it.

'Tell me,' she said. 'Whatever it is, I can handle it. She cancelled their order, but what?'

'It's not her. Tommy came out to the workshop today. He was off school again. I think I told you that. I looked up from my work and he was standing in the doorway looking at me. He looked weird. He's a fierce little bugger sometimes. I was using the new electric planer. I knew he didn't approve of me getting that fucking thing, but I needed it and I thought he'd more or less decided it was okay for me to have it. Anyway, I switched it off and asked him what he was up to. He said, You sold out your dream of being a true craftsman at the first sign of money, Dad.' Tom looked at her. 'It chilled me. The way he said it. Just like that. It really did. Our son is disappointed in his dad.'

She reached and touched his cheek. 'That's not true. He doesn't understand.'

'He will never have faith in me ever again. I know it. You should have seen him. The look he gave me. The way he said it. Jesus! And that fucking woman didn't even have the decency to call me. She sent me a one-line fucking email. Now my son says he's lost faith in his dad.'

'You're taking it too seriously. You're tired. You've drunk a whole bottle of wine. And you're upset. Tommy was just repeating what he's heard from us.'

'You sold out at the first sign of money, Dad? You should have heard him. He was scary. I mean it. It shook me.' He looked at Fran. 'Do you think I've sold out?'

'Oh, for God's sake. Of course you haven't sold out.'

'No. You know what? He's right. I have sold out. I didn't have an answer for him. I've lost his trust. I can't bear to think of it.'

'You're being melodramatic.'

He looked at her, his expression grim. 'Melodramatic?' He lay back heavily against the cushions.

They were silent for some time.

She said, 'Did he tell you about the knife Ina gave him?'

Tom sat up. 'What's that got to do with this?'

'I don't know. I just wondered if you knew.'

'I was with him when she gave it to him. It was Jim's. He has more respect for Ina than he has for me.'

'Don't be silly. You know that's not true. Why are you being so silly about this? Tell him you're just a weak old man who can't help himself. Have a laugh with him. You're being too earnest about it.'

'I'm telling you something that's fucking important to me and you're not taking it seriously. Let's face it, you and I are not exactly communicating tonight.'

'We're both tired and upset. We should talk in the morning.'

'So, what are *you* upset about?'

'You, of course. What did Margie say when you told her they'd cancelled the order?'

'She gave me a beautiful cuddle. She's so incredibly solid, that girl. She's amazing.' He looked at Fran. 'She's a woman already! Can you believe it? Our little Margie is a woman.'

'Yes, she is. The time has passed too quickly.' Fran stretched and leaned against Tom. She said, 'Do you remember that fuss with Claire Pollard last year?'

'The one fighting the charge of bullying?'

'Skänder changed the meeting time and the agenda at the last minute tonight and I had to write and let the other members of staff know. Claire got back to me with a nasty email.' She put her hand on his leg. 'It really pissed me off.'

'You spent days taking care of that woman's case for her. I thought you were her hero.'

'Nobody's a hero in that place. I think I hate her. Do you know what? You were right when you said every farm needs a dog. Tommy needs a dog. Tell him you want to get him a dog. Go with him. Take him along with you. He loves you. You said we need a farm dog. We should take them to Europe while they're still with us. It will be all over otherwise. They'll leave us one of these days and that will be that. We'll be the old couple. It will happen overnight. In a flash. We'll have failed them.' She was seeing Joseph and Eleni struggling across their cosy living room like a couple of helpless drunks. Drunk with old age. Drunk with death.

'That's all bloody years away.'

'So is their babyhood. They were both cuddly little frogs a minute ago, now look at them. I wore this dressing-gown to the hospital for Tommy.'

'That's right. So you did.'

She felt him staring at her. 'What?' she said.

'Something happened in China, didn't it?'

An icy chill shot through her. She closed her eyes.

'I don't want to know about it,' he said. 'But I do want you to know I noticed. We all did. Margie asked me how come things weren't the same with us two.' He laughed. 'Ah well, we've had fourteen good years. What does it say in the Bible? The fat years and the lean years. How many of each are there supposed to be? I guess it's time for the lean years. We've done pretty well really. Better than most, I'd say. You've enjoyed it, haven't you?'

Her thoughts had shot straight to an image of the photograph on the wall behind the bar at the Newstead pub. How many times had she driven past the pub since she got home and tried to make herself go in and look at his picture? She swore she would never look for it. If she saw a snapshot of a man with two people she knew from her real life it would spoil her perfect memory of him forever. It would make it ordinary. How could

Tom know something? She said levelly, 'I was probably away too long. Things weren't quite the same around here when I got back either. Things don't stand still, do they? We all change.' She was afraid she might be overdoing it.

He kept looking at her, saying nothing for quite a time, watching her.

She was terrified of what was about to happen. She would give anything for it not to happen.

Then he said, his voice calm, relaxed, thinking about things, 'It's not the same, though. Is it? I mean, let's face it, it hasn't been the same since you got back. The kids noticed. It's not just me.'

She drank the rest of the wine in her glass and stood up. Then she sat down again.

He said, 'It's okay! Whatever it was, it's okay. I shouldn't have said anything. You're right. The boy needs a dog. I'll take him with me and he can choose a pup. It's true. He needs a playmate. A farm isn't a farm without a dog. I promised myself I wouldn't mention this China business. Buying that bloody electric planer has unsettled me. I've let you all down. I've let myself down.' He laughed. 'Making all that fuss about being a fucking craftsman of the old school. Jesus! What a load of shit.' He smiled. 'You're living with a failure, Dr Frances Egan!'

'You're not a failure.' Her voice came to her from a long way off.

'I couldn't bear it if I lost you.'

'You're not going to lose me.' Had he already lost her? What did it mean, to lose someone?

'When you were away in China I couldn't sleep. It was like I was getting a message. I panicked one night. I just knew I'd lost you. It wasn't a dream. It was this dread. It just whacked me.' He looked at her, a sharp, quick look, something coming into his mind. 'Do you believe in telepathy between people who are really close?'

'We all need a break,' she said. 'We can take the kids to Europe during the long vac. I'll ask the dean to let me take some of my accrued leave. He can't refuse. Three months. If he makes a fuss, I'll talk to HR and say I'm stressed. The kids need to see Europe with us. Your mother would be over the moon if we spent a few weeks with her. How long is it since she's seen them?'

He rested back against the cushions. 'A holiday like that will cost a bomb. We were going to use that money to finish the kitchen and bathroom in the cottage.'

'We'll use it for us. Restoring the cottage can wait. There's no hurry for that. But the children will be grown up in a couple of years.'

'I'd love to see Mum before she goes.' He turned his head and smiled at her. 'You're perfect, you know that? Bloody perfect.' He kept looking at her. 'I want you.'

She didn't say anything. The ground had been snatched out from under her. She didn't know the limits. What was Tom really saying? What could he possibly know? Everything she loved would be destroyed. Undone. Shattered. Her marriage would be reduced to a farce. Trust! Everything they'd built. China had made it all so terribly vulnerable. But even while her terror had possession of her, she knew that if she were to see him again, she would make love with him. She did not regret it. It still astonished her. Had she discovered with him who she really was? Was that it? I am that woman! I am! She closed her eyes.

'What about the chooks?' he said.

Does he know? How could he know? No one knows!

'Who's going to feed them while we're over there giving the kids a look at the civilised world?'

She had to make an effort. It was a game, wasn't it? It wasn't reality. Was it? 'Ina will be delighted if you ask her. You've done lots of things for Ina. Tommy loves her. He told me his plan is to live in her cottage after she's dead. He thinks you're going to bury her in her orchard. I've missed out on all this. I'm not part of it.'

'Ina is a woman who has little to say.'

'I suppose at her age there's nothing much left to say.'

'She's intelligent. I like her a lot. She's completely dependable. That's the feeling I get with her.'

'She's lived alone up there on those five acres with her goats and her kitchen garden and her dog since her husband died. For Tommy she's the old woman who lives forever. Little Tommy thinks she has always been as she is today, the old woman on the ridge. He's written a story about her. He's never let any of us see any of his stories, but he's given a story to Ina. Did you know that?'

'Yes. I knew it.'

She was thinking, He will bring it up again one day. Or later tonight. Now that he's mentioned it, it will be in the air between us, waiting for its moment to explode in our faces. Or it will seep out. I'll just tell him. No! No, I'll never tell him. He will bring it up again when he's feeling depressed and angry with himself. He will fire it at me. Just like that. Out of the blue. Did you fuck someone over there in China? I'll lie to him. Then there will be this lie between us. It will corrode our trust. Has it already corroded our trust? Isn't not telling him the same as lying to him? Or worse? I'm definitely not going to tell him! It's mine. It's not his. I don't regret it. It's the only thing I have that is really and truly just mine and no one else's. My own private secret thing that has nothing to do with my family or my job or anything except the two of us. If I were to tell him, then all this would be at an end and that would no longer be sacred. That word we use! Sacred. Nothing is really sacred. We're hypocrites. All of us. Silence will preserve it. To speak of its mystery will be to deny the mystery. The mystery is in the silence. I must keep that. That's what's sacred: the silence. It's always the silence in the end. Once we speak of something, our words change it. It loses its simplicity. It becomes something else. It would no longer be mine. It would become ours. Our problem. She looked at him. He looked tired. She felt sorry for him. Losing the splendid order from that woman was awful for him. If I were to tell him about Hefei he would be understanding. It would be horrible. Deep down he would be humiliated and I would owe him my understanding. It would become a nest of disease and worry between us. There would be no way for us to deal with it. It would crush him. I would watch his imagination taking him to it whenever he wanted sex and I would see how he had learned to hate me. He would deny it. He would go into denial. And, slowly, we would decay. We would all begin to feel it, the truth, that we were living in a hollow shell. We would all be lost. It would break us. We're already too old to ever get over it. The two realities would cancel each other out. There would be nothing left if I ever let the truth come between us. The lie is a necessity if we are to survive.

'I'm going to bed.' She stood up. One day she would be like Eleni, stumbling and clawing her way around the furniture, her body tormented. That is the reward at the end of the struggle. A struggle we can't win. A couple more quick decades and we'll be there. I will never share my secret. My secret will give me the strength to endure. I will take it whole and perfect with me to my grave. I will never tell Tom. No one would ever really understand something like that about another person, except maybe Valerie, a woman like Valerie, a woman who understands the tragic poetry of our lives. A woman who can voice the mystery without explaining it. But she is dead. Valerie is beyond the reach of the living. Safely dead. Fran sat down again.

They sat in the silence.

She thought, There are moments when making love with my Mongolian warrior in the hotel room in Hefei has made me the loneliest woman in the world. She stood up again and picked up her glass.

Tom was watching her. He said, 'Maybe I could sell the planer and redeem myself in my son's eyes. What do you reckon? Maybe that bitch cancelling the job did me a good turn after all?' He watched Fran going over to the sink, where she stood rinsing her wineglass then drying it carefully on a tea towel. 'You're an amazing woman! I don't deserve you. Will we have to be evicted from this little bit of paradise of ours?'

She turned and looked at him. Why did he say that? She dried the glass. He shouldn't have said anything. When you put something into words, it changes it and then you're wrestling with your need to know more and your dread of knowing more. It's already eating him. Doubt, that's what it is. Once doubt gets in it's like damp in the walls, rising damp from the earth. You can never stop it.

Tom stood up and went over to the Ned Kelly and closed the damper. The fire would slumber until morning. 'I'll ask the dealer in Ballarat to sell the fucking thing. I'll take a loss and start again. Cleanly. I'll stick to using Grandad's old hand tools. Tommy will forgive me. He'll see that his old man is human after all.' He looked at his watch. 'Do you realise it's half past midnight?'

She was looking out of the kitchen window. The moon had risen. The night was beautiful. Solitary. The darkness a lovely perfection. *When I look at the moon I shall think of you.*

He said, 'I'm on the cusp of being old. Fifty in a blink from now. I don't deserve all this. Margie's already thinking of boys. The next thing she'll be sneaking out to meet up with some hoon in his car.' He carried the two empty wine bottles and his glass through to the kitchen. He put the bottles and the glass down by the sink and put his arms around Fran's waist from behind and held himself against her, resting his head on her shoulder. 'I think I'm depressed.' He said this quietly, his mouth close to her ear, confiding. 'I don't really mind all that much, so long as you don't mind. Do you think you can handle it? God, I love your smell. You are my smell of home.'

She covered his hands with her own where they were gripping her belly. 'I love this place. That bird! You stop hearing it after a while. It gives us back the silence.'

The old stone cottage down the hill shone in the moonlight, the windows reflecting the cold white light. 'There's plenty of time to finish doing up the cottage. We're still young. There's no hurry.' She turned around, holding him away and examining him. 'So you turned out to be a hopeless, depressed failure.' She laughed. There was an odd little touch of sadness in her laugh, a touch of the truth. The truth was closely wrapped in that touch of sadness. She could not share it. The truth will find a way, she thought. 'And you're an idiot as well. I don't know what I ever saw in you, Thomas Green.' They held each other close. Then, slowly, they kissed. It turned into a long kiss. It went on and on. There was a lot to express.

It was probably expecting too much from one kiss between two people who had been living together for fourteen years. But they gave it a go. Nothing's perfect, after all. And Tom was right, it wasn't quite the same, but it still worked a touch of the old magic, just enough, and they turned out the light and went to bed and made love, the way people do, imperfectly, and they slept and woke again in the morning to another day of hopes and disappointments and strange disfigurements of the truth, some of which they shared with each other and with the children and some of which they kept to themselves. And it was Tom who, on Saturday morning over breakfast, while he made pancakes and they all sat at the table waiting for them, announced to the children that they were all going to Europe at the end of the year and they had to choose which country they wanted to see.

Margie said, 'I'll go where you go, Dad. And can we also go to Paris? I want to see the Mona Lisa. Is it in Paris?'

Little Tommy said he would stay with Ina while they were away, but they shouted him down.

Margie clipped him over the ear so that he yelped. 'Don't be an idiot! You want to go to the Natural History Museum in London. You know you do. You can send Ina a postcard.'

Tom himself wanted to go to Somerset to see his mother and to visit the workshops of craftsmen and women who had stuck to their adzes and awls. 'I'll go back to basics and start again.'

Then they all looked at Fran.

Little Tommy said, 'You haven't said where you want to go, Mum.'

'I was just thinking. Maybe we could make a quick visit to Ireland to see my mother.'

'I'll go to Ireland with you,' Tommy said.

Would her mother want to see her?

Tom set down the large plate piled with pancakes. They were all forking pancakes onto their plates and waiting impatiently for their turn at the maple syrup.

Fran said, 'And I'd like to go to Tunisia too. Perhaps while you're in Somerset seeing your mother.'

After breakfast little Tommy went back to writing his secret stories and his big sister went and lay on her bed and thought her secret thoughts and gazed out from her bedroom window towards the old lady's cottage on the ridge, a look of infinitely gentle melancholy in her beautiful grey eyes. Even if she had wished to, and she did not just then wish to, Margie would not have been able to share her emotion with her parents or her brother. Her truth was too big to share now. And she didn't understand it. She did not know what the emotion she was feeling really was. She had no word for it, just the feeling of it. It gave to her perfect features an elusive beauty that an artist in the olden days might have been inspired to immortalise, back when artists thought beauty worth immortalising, so long ago no one remembers it anymore.

Then reality did its little trick and the moment was gone, and it was Monday morning again and Margie was getting on the school bus and waving out the window to her father as the bus drew away. Her friend leaned into her and said, 'I like your dad.' Margie smiled and murmured, 'He's lovely,' and there was a tear in her eye as she said it. She was thinking about her father's vulnerability and the retired brain surgeon cancelling the order for a dining suite, the order that had been such a wonderful thing to happen to him and a real vote of confidence in his craftsman's skills.

Then the bus drove away and Tom's HiLux did a U-turn and headed back towards the farm. And then the country road by the school bus stop was empty again, except for the family of magpies that were finding succulent insects among the grass and weeds along the verges, warbling and squabbling over this and that and carrying on like a real family themselves, the day warming up after the chilly night, the sky clear and the paddocks with their grazing cattle and sheep bordered by belts of box ironbark forest. After the magpies flew off, the only movement was an echidna crossing the stretch of bitumen and everything else was much as it usually was, with no great heart-stopping event to report and little more to wish for.

'So why Tunisia?' Tom asked her after quite a long silence between them. Coming after the silence, his question sounded a bit abrupt to Fran and she thought she detected an undertone of irritation in it, as if he'd been sitting there mulling it over in his head for some time, complicating its meaning for himself in that slightly paranoid way he'd got into, before finally blurting it out. She thought, Yes, why Tunisia, but why the irritation?

They were sitting side by side on the couch facing the wood heater. They had been drinking the heavy red wine they both liked. It was late now. It was their special time of the evening to be together, without the children and without their work, just the two of them as they used to be, as they had been for that brief time before they were married and had children, a time when they were both still passionately interested to know what the other one was thinking and feeling, when they had picnicked on the grass in the botanical gardens on summer days and he had rested his head in her lap and looked up into her eyes, desiring and puzzling and adoring. A time when they were telling each other their dreams, his hope of establishing himself as a fine cabinet-maker of the old school, and her dream of becoming a professor. A time now long before the labyrinth of complicated moods and uncertainties, and the more difficult familiarity of routine, had woven their web.

Watching her reading Valerie's diary earlier, he had said he would be interested to hear her read something from it. Which wasn't quite what he'd meant. What he'd really meant, but didn't want to say in so many words, because saying it would be bound to make it real, was, Why are you keeping her diary so bloody secret? We used to share everything. We aren't sharing things anymore the way we used to. That's one real change since China.

It was true. She didn't want to share Valerie's diary with him. But whether the need to keep things to herself had begun since China, or was already there when she arrived in China, she couldn't say. She wondered if it was the need to have something of her own that had made her slide so effortlessly into her brief affair with the beautiful man on the bus. Would she have fallen in love that night in Hefei if she'd not already been feeling this need for something of her own?

Fran took another drink of wine then she set the glass down on the low table in front of the couch and she picked up Valerie's diary, which she had put down by this time on the couch beside her, and she opened the diary and read to him from the section that would answer his question.

He listened without interrupting her, resting back against the cushions and gazing straight ahead at the dull red glow from the dying fire behind the window of the Ned Kelly. He needed to be reassured that there was nothing difficult or disturbing lurking between them. Since she'd got home from China he'd had the feeling things had changed between them, almost as if there was a stranger in the house with them whose presence neither of them was allowed to mention.

She could feel his nagging need to be reassured by her, so before beginning to read to him, she placed her hand on his thigh and leaned across and kissed him on the mouth.

He smiled and put his arms around her and he whispered, 'God, I love you!'

'I love you too,' she said. And it was true. She did love him. But she was more aware these days that there were many different ways of loving. She read the entry slowly, and Tom gazed into the fire and listened.

The entry she read was from a time before Valerie arrived at Caloola, during the years when she was in England living with her father's sister, Phillipa Sommers.

Sidi Bou Said, Tunisia, July 1947

My twenty-first birthday yesterday. The best birthday present ever! I love Aunt Phillipa! Who would take her for my cold father's sister? She is so calm and so sure of her purpose, so open and so generous. I hope I can be like her one day. I don't believe in God anymore, of course, but all the same I shall ask him to make me like Aunt Phillipa. You never know—perhaps he really does exist and will do it for me. Wave his magic wand, and I shall begin to shine as she shines, with a light of real enthusiasm that knows nothing of the cruelty of doubt.

The evening is the best time here. During the day it is too hot to venture outside. Now, in the evening, the smell of jasmine comes in the great window and fills my room with its sweetness. I sit on the cool stone of the sill and lean my back against the deep wall. The iron belly of the window's defences makes a fretwork of the evening sky. The last blade of hot light is painted along the western horizon beyond the garden wall. Surely this is a place to live and a place to die. It is my greatest regret that I do not belong here. That is the source of my present sadness. For where do I belong?

Why must there always be this feeling of loss? And then the beauty arises. At first there is only the sound of the water trickling from the fountain's head into the stone basin in the centre of the courtyard outside my door. It is the coolest sound imaginable. I wish I could find the poetry of it, but no word has come to me. Arising from the silence of the fountain, I think at first it is the sound of a woman weeping, a lamentation, and I ask myself is it her despair for the death of her child or her lover? The woman's lamentation rises and falls, is like the softly rolling waves on a distant shore, as if it will never cease. I listen, and am lulled and enclosed by it. The woman is singing an old song that belongs to her soul, to the soul of her people. The song is so ancient there is no time in it but only the immeasurable tone of its eternity; it sings of death and life and the enduring sea. It belongs to her. Straining to hear the last moment of her song, it is I who knows that she has fallen silent, her voice replaced once again by the tinkling vanity of the fountain. I wait for her to begin again, the air expectant, the strain of her absence mounting in me deliciously, then a low-toned drum begins to beat, slowly, softly, itself a distant echo of her

lamentation returned from those remote tidal sweeps of its
infinitely distant shores, and then her voice rises once again
from the well of her belief and is carried by the rhythm of
the drum. It is so beautiful that I weep. My heart's tears
are hot and run down my cheeks unchecked and I long
to enter her song with her but I cannot. And that is when
I begin to know my own sorrow, my loss.

I have no song of my own. The link is broken. I am
from a broken tribe.

My aunt works at repairing the chasm in us but it will
not mend. I am lost in the empty wilderness without my
song. The song of my people. I have no people. I listen
to the woman singing her antique song and I learn of
my own irreparable loss. Now she is joined by one of her
companions, the two voices striking out like swimmers
into familiar rhythms, unafraid, uplifted, defended always
against the terror of uncertainty and the deep solitariness
of the human soul, until five or six voices are joined
together and the loneliness is defeated and driven away and
they are the voices of women who are one.

Aunt Phillipa has learned their language and their
customs and has written numerous books about these
women and their supremely confident culture that gives
them the strength to withstand the tragedy of their situation. When she was young, she asked a friend among

them to teach her their songs so that she could join
with them. But her first and dearest friend among them
put her hand on her arm and told her, 'It is not given to us
to sing another's song.'

Aunt Phillipa knew at once the truth of this. So, she
gave up trying to become a Berber woman and decided
to be content with being their champion in a world
indifferent to their cruel fate. 'It was the best I could do,'
she said to me, giving me her lovely warm smile, her arm
light and companionable around my shoulders. I don't
want her to take her arm away. I want the moment to last
forever. We were sitting on the terrace that overlooks the
town below and the sun was setting.

'To know who one is not,' she said to me that evening,
'is a truer wisdom than to know who one is. They have
given me freely all that can be given to a stranger with the
open generosity of all peoples who still know themselves,
but they cannot give me their song, for it is in their song
that they give voice to their old gods, and their melancholy
becomes a celebration. We feel it with them and our hearts
are moved. But we cannot be them. We cannot be who
we are not. For us, the old link is broken. That is our
tragedy. We have lost our beginnings. We have abandoned
our old gods who taught us to celebrate the gift of life,
and we are frowned upon by the one true God. We can

no longer sing our old song and our universe has become a place of fear and uncertainty.

'Once, long ago, so long ago we have lost even our legends of it, our meaning resided confidently within the song of our old gods. When that link was broken, our brief moment out of the eternity of silence, our moment between our birth and our death, became at once filled with a frantic search for our lost meaning. It was in the lost song of the gods that we had once known our consolation. The rest is vanity, the rest is uncertainty and fear, we die with the question unanswered, still on our lips. We are ruled, and there is no consolation for us.'

She laughed and embraced me and we drank the wine.

'So, I became a philosopher,' she said and laughed again, and she flung her powerful body's weight against the back of the cane chair and made an ample gesture with her free arm, sweeping across the deep view over the ancient landscape. 'Did you know this house was once the palace of the local Ottoman bey? When the Ottomans abandoned North Africa it was the Christian White Fathers who took it over and used it as a religious house. And it was they, their astonishing leader, a Frenchman, who gave this house to the lost Berber women who once led their caravans across the desert wearing their riches openly on their headdresses, boldly refusing the veil, as they do today. We have so much to learn from them. Whoever is intact can teach us everything we wish to know.'

So it is here, in this house of the lost women of the desert, that I discover in the mysterious beauty of their song why I am alone and lost, and it is Aunt Phillipa who gives me her strength to see and to understand and joins me with her generous spirit.

Fran rested back against the couch and closed her eyes. Outside, the bird sent its signal into the night. She could never really share Valerie's secret thoughts with him. They were like her own secret thoughts.

Tom sat up. 'Thank you, darling. That was beautiful. I love the way you read. You really mean it. You don't hurry through it. You read as if you want it to be true.' He leaned and kissed her on the lips. 'Do you think you'll write something about her?'

'I don't know. I might.' How impossible it is to share some things. She was seeing Valerie in the old bey's palace in Sidi Bou Said, the antique song of the women rising and falling, a lamentation and a celebration, a song of their common reality, the source of their certainty. 'I would like to inhabit her world,' she said. 'Just a little. I want to go there and at least see how it is today. If there is anything left of what she found there. Perhaps I can meet some Berber women. I don't know. I have no idea.

It might be a mistake. But I'd just like to follow her tracks a little way and see where they lead me.' She looked at him.

'It's a lovely idea. It's *you*. You know that. Your eyes shine when you talk about Valerie and her life. She suffered, didn't she? I mean, it can't have been a lot of fun for her living out there in that nut house back then.'

The diary had been an invitation to open herself up to something that had always been in her. It still astonished her that Joseph had given it to her at just the right moment. 'Three years ago, I would have looked at it and put it aside without recognising it,' she said. 'Then, if I were to pick it up again in twenty or thirty years' time, when it was too late, I'd have seen what a beautiful offer was in it and how I'd missed it. How sad would that be? It must happen. That we are so preoccupied with the hustle of the everyday we miss the one thing that's right for us.'

He surprised her when he said, 'You've always been a bit inspired by the melancholy of things.'

She looked at him. 'Of things?'

'Of life.' He smiled. 'I do love you, you know.'

'I know you do.'

'Don't stay too long in Tunisia, will you?'

She was aware that Valerie's humanity was warmer than her own. It was richer. More rounded and full. She said, 'My sense of reality is cold and narrow compared to Valerie's. Reading her makes me realise my inner life is half empty.' She laughed, trying to make light of it.

'There's nothing cold and narrow about you, Dr Egan. You are warm and you're a believer in people. And I'm one of your followers, you've always been our leader.'

She laughed. 'Margie doesn't think so.'

'Margie's a bit awed by you, that's all. She feels safer with me.'

'Do you think so?'

'Margie isn't going to have to be like her dad. There's no pressure on her.'

'Do I put pressure on her?'

'Just being you. She looks at you and it makes her wonder about her own womanhood. She's only just coming into herself. She's meeting herself for the first time and it's like meeting a stranger. We all felt that way, didn't we? Some get lost trying to deal with it. Margie's basically strong and hopeful and she knows we both love her to bits. It's herself she doubts, not us. The stranger in her.' He looked at her. 'We all went through that, didn't we?'

'You hardly ever talk like this.'

'She's becoming more like you.' He grinned. 'Do daughters always become their mothers in the end?'

'I never really liked my mother. It sounds terrible, doesn't it? Of course I loved her. You can't help loving your mother. But I never liked her. I mean, good on her for doing her own thing and going home to Ireland when Dad died, but she's always been so bloody negative about everything. If I ever said I was going to do something, she'd turn up her nose and say, Why don't you do what Alice Rivers did? Now there's a girl who knows what she's about. In the end I just stopped telling her what I was thinking. If I told her something, she spoiled it. She couldn't help herself. She didn't know how to help me celebrate my ideas.'

She got up off the couch and went over to the stove and held her hands out to the warm iron. The fire had burned down. The room was cooling. 'I don't want to grow old not having tried.'

'What about your career?'

'I don't know. I don't know. We don't always have to know, do we? Who says we have to know? We don't need to understand everything. Things aren't as clear for me as they were when I was younger. That's all.'

'You're still young.'

'Younger.' She was thinking of her colleagues. They'd become shrivelled caricatures of their old selves during the past few years, her hopes and expectations for them in ruins. She thought of Claire Pollard's nastiness. Claire used to be such an open happy person. A good person. Reliably good. The place had shrunk her. She'd become mean. Holding on for dear life to what was left of it, what was left of her dreams. All rancid and stale and impossible. Never to be fulfilled. It was the place.

Fran felt only revulsion at the idea of going in there every day; the idea of becoming herself yet another professor was repulsive to her. Surely she had seen in Valerie's diary the truth that what Tom called her career was a trap under these conditions, baited with the promise of a miserable professorship at the end of it. For years she had fallen for that delusion, the great career! It would suffocate her. She felt it whenever she saw Skänder or the ghastly Eric Thornton. They frightened her. They were blind to the things that Valerie had valued, the things she herself loved. She had ceased to draw any sustenance from her career. Those people weren't interested in educating the young. They had no interest in education. To become one of them would kill her hopes of ever achieving anything beautiful and true in her own life. To become a professor would be the sound of the key turning in the lock. Her own death rattle. She laughed and looked at Tom. 'What?' He was watching her.

He said quietly, 'China, eh? We started along a new path after you got back. Wouldn't you say? We both seem to have recognised something that we just weren't dealing with before.'

She stood looking down at him for some time, saying nothing. Then she said, 'Maybe.' But he was right. It *was* China. China had been the opening. Jargal Batu. She said, 'I'm forty-two. There is so much more. I feel as if there is another life out there. I want to get to know myself more fully. I don't want to be locked in. I want to become more me. There is more of me.'

Tom got up and came over and stood close beside her. 'Let me get a bit of old Ned's warmth.'

'Does that sound silly?'

'Not to me. I know you. You're a slow burn. People who don't know you might say, But she's already got everything. A lovely home and a family and a successful career. What's her problem?'

'But you don't say that? You don't secretly think it, do you? Valerie speaks about the beauty and the tragedy. She speaks in the deeper tones of a life that inhabits an emotional land-scape far richer than mine. We're not just one person, are we? There are truer selves we find and which fit us more honestly than the old selves that once seemed to be us. Like dresses or shoes. It's not just a meaningless coincidence that Joseph found Valerie Sommers's diary and gave it to me after I'd been to China. Joseph's timing was perfect. That's fate, isn't it? I think I believe in fate. Not Fate with a capital F but the reality of perfect coincidences that help us become more fully ourselves. It's a search, after all. I mean, we're not born knowing who we are. Our fate helps us become more liberally ourselves. I don't mean a mysterious guiding hand, just productive coincidence. Let's call it that for now; Fate with a capital F is too difficult these days.'

* * *

Lying in bed later, wide awake beside Tom, she returned to their conversation and to her memory. If Jargal Batu had said to her that night in the hotel room in Hefei, This is love, isn't it? she would have replied, Yes, that is what this is. How to tell Tom that? *She* understood it. *She* believed it. But how to justify such things to someone else, even to someone you loved, as she loved Tom? There was a limit. That night in Hefei she was not the mother her children knew. They would not have known her. And if she were to bring it all out and lay it before Tom, he would get tangled up in the net of it. They both would. What a mess it would be. A bomb would go off and blow them apart. Blow them to bits. Body parts. The plain truth would become something untrue. The truth was too much. That was the trouble. We can't have the truth. Who can live with it? The facts are too bitter. We're better off without it, without them. Things are possible without the truth. With it, nothing would ever hold together for long. Especially not marriage. Once it gets into your head, truth is a carnivore lodged in the brain. It eats its way into everything. How would you ever get it out again once it had made its fatal entry into you? You would be eaten up by it day and night. We live by the myth, not by the truth. Our lovely, private, cosy, reassuring myths. Our hopeless dreams. We need them the way we needed our teddy when we were little kids. Teddy understood us as no one else ever understood us. Teddy was perfect. Teddy was not the truth. Teddy was make-believe. Perfect make-believe. We loved him. We must take care of Teddy. We must take care of our make-believe.

Fran must have gone to sleep then, for the next thing she knew she was swimming far out on her own in the Indian Ocean and didn't know which way was home. She woke gasping for air, thinking of Tom saying to her, It was idealism that got you into teaching. You wanted to help the kids in the northern suburbs. What happened to that? And her response, It's sick. The whole system is sick. It's about funding. We're managers, not educators. Managers and fundraisers. Education has become irrelevant to the system. They just want the money. We are obsessed with funding shortfalls. The idealism is still in me. I still feel it. It's there, but there's no place for it at the university. It's me I need now, not idealism. She wasn't able to get back to sleep.

She got up and made a cup of tea and stood in the kitchen drinking the tea and eating Granita biscuits from the packet. It was three o'clock. The moon had gone over to the other side of the house. A fox was walking calmly across the open space just beyond the deck where the shadow of the roof line ended and the moonlight began. The fox stopped to investigate the barbecue. It was without colour. A soft black shadow moving in the night. She had research funds that would pay for a replacement to take her teaching load for the first semester. Tom wanted to spend Christmas with his mother in Somerset.

She'd take three or four months of her long-service leave. They'd be away for the European winter and home in time for the Australian autumn.

She was getting cold standing at the window. She went back to the bedroom and got into the bed beside Tom. He was snoring, his left arm flung out. She lifted his arm out of the way. The sheets on her side of the bed were cold. The thought of visiting her mother in Ballyragget made her nervous. Nothing was simple. Would she even go there? She snuggled across to share a little of Tom's warmth. 'My Tom,' she said softly, to reassure herself, to hear the meaning in it, the claim. He turned and put his arm over her. He was still asleep. His breath was sour. He was drinking too much lately. She would have to tell him about it again. His belief in the perfecting of their love over the years, as if they were two identical trees that would gradually grow together until they were eventually indistinguishable from each other, all that had oppressed her. The whole idea of it. She couldn't believe in something like that. The perfection of love over time. It was a nonsense. It was avoiding the simple complicated truth. Tom was an idealist about love and marriage. He was reliably himself. He grew older but he didn't change. Tom was content with being himself. He would always be who he was now. She couldn't be like that. For years she had tried to be one person, and it had made her unhappy. In Hefei she had discovered beyond any doubt that she was more than one person. She could not now unlearn that. She couldn't pretend it hadn't happened and was not as real for her as was being the mother of her children.

THREE

Fran parked under a plane tree on the opposite side of the road from the entrance gates. She switched off the engine and sat looking along the driveway into the grounds. The side portion of what was evidently a grand residence was visible to her. The main section of the house was obscured by a dense copse of old elms and oaks. The day was grey, overcast and windblown, autumn leaves gathering in the gutters. The first of May already and a foretaste of another Melbourne winter. It had been spring in Paris. The heavy timber gates were open, branches from wild-grown thickets of cotoneaster poking through the bars, hydrangea bushes further along the drive still carrying the russet dead heads of last season's blooms. The place appeared to be deserted. Abandoned. Awaiting the developer with his bulldozer and his plans.

She picked up the diary from the seat beside her and put it in her bag. She stepped out of the car and locked it, then stood resting her back against the car, buttoning her overcoat and looking along the quiet street. The old plane trees meeting overhead created the impression of an enclosed avenue. There was no traffic. The rich lived here in their quiet tree-lined streets. They were not to be seen. She walked across the road and went in through the gates and along the driveway, the gravel crunching under her shoes, the trees and shrubs to either side of her thrashing in the cold wind. She was nervous and not sure what she would say if she were challenged by a security guard. Several ornately patterned brick chimneys came into view over to her right, rising self-importantly from the complex of roof lines on the main house. An iron fountain in the centre of what had once been a lawn was filled with dead sticks and leaves. When she drew level with the front entrance, she saw that a minor offshoot of the main driveway continued on along the left-hand side of the house. She caught a whiff of cigarette smoke, then it was gone. There must be someone about.

She stood at the junction, not sure which way to go, the wind tugging at her, her hair across her eyes. She went on along the offshoot and soon came in sight of the side door of the house. Facing the door, on the other side of the path, was an unpainted timber shed. The shed was overgrown by a tangled rosebush. The embrace of the rose had grappled the shed into a sideways lean, pieces of the weatherboard sprung and hanging off, the old nails like little black teeth in the hard light. The shed door was open. It moved back and forth a little at each gust of wind that burst down the side of the house. Fran turned her back on the shed and got out her mobile and took a photo of the side door, with its ornate little porch. She wasn't really sure what she was doing there. She had been expecting to find the judge's old house, where Valerie was born. Now that she was at Valerie's childhood home, it wasn't possible to imagine the woman who had written the diary living here. Valerie in her haunted office out at the university, or sitting in the sun by the apple tree in the asylum garden watching the rainbow lorikeets: they were real to her, but there was nothing in the diary about this house that might have made the place familiar for her.

She was looking down at the photo of the door on her phone, not sure what she would do next, when a sound like a shoe scraping against a board made her turn around.

An old woman stood in the open doorway of the shed. She was stooped and was carrying a rusty bucket with a bunch of dry sticks poking out of it. Her other hand she rested on an elaborate metal walking aid. A modern device, the walking aid had four short legs at the bottom, angled out to spread the load. The woman's thin hair was long and without colour and blew freely across her face, her pale scalp visible. A lighted cigarette hung from her lips. The skin of her cheeks was pale and deeply lined. She was thin, the bones of her shoulders prominent under a dirty old mackintosh. 'You're wasting your time,' she said. 'It's not for sale! I've told you people that before.'

'I'm sorry. I thought the house was deserted. I wasn't thinking it might be for sale.'

'What do you want? I'm in the phone book. Doesn't anyone have the courtesy these days to call and make an appointment? You'd better leave before I let the dogs out. Toby and Demeter don't like strangers.' The cigarette waggled up and down between her lips when she spoke. The action of the cigarette reminded Fran of the way she had seen women smoking in Paris, as if to smoke were a mark of distinction, the sign of an independent spirit, women prepared to blow their smoke in your face and make no apology for it. She had felt a mild envy of them.

'Can I ask you, is this the house that once belonged to Judge Sommers?'

'Who wants to know?'

'I'm interested in finding out about his daughter, Valerie. My name is Frances Egan. I was given something personal that once belonged to the judge's daughter. I couldn't help being interested.' She hesitated. 'I don't suppose by any chance you knew her?'

'Nobody knew Valerie Sommers.' She gave a throaty laugh, the cigarette miraculously staying put between her lips. 'Valerie Sommers didn't even know herself.'

The old woman turned around and reached for the knob of the shed door and tugged at it. The door moved an inch or two before the bottom caught against the tilt of the floor and resisted. She let it go with an impatient flinging gesture of the hand and stepped out onto the pathway. She stood on the path and breathed, sucking the end of the cigarette. 'So what's this personal thing you've been given?'

'It's a diary. It was rescued from the workmen by our caretaker out at the university. He thought I'd be interested. And I am.'

'Show me!' The old woman set down the bucket and reached out. 'We're from the same planet, Frances Egan. Just show me!'

Fran took the diary out of her bag. She held it close, unwilling to let it go.

'I'm Valerie Sommers. Show me the diary.'

It was a shock. Could this derelict old woman really be Valerie? She must be nearly ninety. Eighty-six or -seven at least.

Frances held out the diary. The old woman took it and stood looking at the stained cover. She set the walking aid aside and opened the book and began reading, her lips moving, the cigarette nodding. She whispered a name, a soft hiss on her lips: 'Jessie!' She looked up. 'Who gave it to you? This was stolen from my room.' She looked down at the open book. She looked up again at Fran. 'Who gave it to you?' Her tone was accusing, as if she suspected Fran of getting hold of the diary by some underhand means. Her eyes were watery and rimmed with a painful-looking redness, sharpened into a squint, either from the smoke or with dislike, or perhaps with tears.

'Our caretaker at the university,' Fran said. 'Joseph Bayer. He saved it from the men renovating the cells.'

'That would be Joseph. He loved to rescue things, and people. So Joseph is still out there?'

'He remembers you.'

'Joseph was my friend.' She said this sternly, as if still needing to rebuke Fran. She was reading from the diary again. Every few lines she exclaimed quietly, 'Oh God!' And then, 'Jessie!' Her voice was soft and private, the wind gusts snatching at her hair, snatching the smoke from her cigarette. She turned aside and spat the cigarette from between her lips. The wind took it and it landed among the weeds at the side of the path, a last gasp of smoke whipped away between the bending dock leaves. She closed the diary and grabbed onto the walking aid, then turned and made the two steps to the side door of the house. She turned the knob and went in and slammed the door behind her.

Fran was dumbfounded. She stood there staring at the door. Was that it? She'd handed the diary back to the old woman?

She had lost it! She felt a surge of resentment. There was no way for her to feel right about this abrupt end to the meeting. She looked at the bucket of dry sticks, which Valerie had left sitting in the middle of the path. This was not going to happen! She went over and picked up the bucket and stepped to the door and banged on it. Three loud bangs that could not be ignored, even by a half-deaf old woman. She was not going to let the diary go just like that. She stood waiting, then banged again and called loudly, 'You forgot your bucket of kindling!'

She stepped back a pace from the door and looked along the wall. Was this really the house in which Valerie's mother had killed herself? If that old woman in there really was Valerie Sommers, why was she living down the back end of her father's old place? The house must be worth a mint.

The door opened. The old woman stood there. 'What do you want?'

'You forgot your bucket.'

The old woman's face was crumpled and stained with tears. She looked wretched. Fran noticed she was not holding the diary. She must have left it inside, as if that was now where it belonged.

Valerie Sommers stood in the doorway staring at Fran as if wondering who she was. Then she said with feeling, 'I should thank you. That little book is very dear to me. I never gave up hope of seeing it again.' She was lost for words for a moment, her lips sucking and her jaw making chewing movements. 'I knew I'd be reunited with it one day. I just knew it.' She shook her head. 'Who did you say you were?'

'I'm Frances Egan. I'm head of the School of Management at Western University.'

'I've never heard of it.'

'We took over the buildings that were once the mental hospital. Caloola.'

'So you're from the madhouse. One of them. I can't talk to you. I'm too upset.' She stood looking at Fran. Then she turned around and would have gone in and closed the door again but she arrested her turn and said, 'I'm in the phone book, Miss Egan. You can call me next week. I will thank you then.' She went in and closed the door.

Fran set the bucket of sticks down and stood looking at the closed door, the cold wind tugging at her coat. There was nothing to be done. She walked back up to the main drive, the bushes lashing at each other like strangers fighting. She went out the gates and crossed the road and climbed into the Renault and started the engine. Before she drove away she looked across at the house, an emptiness in her mind now where the diary had been, the companionship of Valerie's intimate voice in that little book, the magic of it, the voice of her own interior life, the voice of the unspoken, the silence of her dreams in the turmoil of Valerie's young life. She knew that woman of the diary. The old woman in that house was not her but was a stranger.

She drove towards the city. The Valerie of the diary was not the old woman to whom she had just relinquished it. 'Well, it's gone,' she said aloud, and she swung the wheel and entered the northbound on-ramp and knitted herself into the speeding traffic.

S he stepped out of the lift and walked to the end of the reception area. Her heart was heavy with resentment, the
expectation of this meeting, the loss of her song, that was how
she had thought of it as she stood in the empty lift rising to the
top floor of the city campus building where the senior boys all
had their eyries. What else wasn't really her own? She was five
minutes early. She could have decided just then to turn around
and hit the down button and leave and never come back. But
she lacked the conviction for that. She stood at the big window
and looked out over the city. The clouds were broken, the grey
day breaking up, patches of sunlight racing across the distant
suburbs, glinting on the river below, tourist boats sliding by,

men and women leaning and rowing in skiffs, the cafes and shops on the south shore busy with people, the tall apartment buildings beyond the Arts Centre reflecting the sun, the golden glass on one of them, the Domain over to the left, the cool green sweep of mown grass and the old trees, a statue of some important bygone man, trams lined up along St Kilda Road. The traffic was at a standstill. A pigeon on the window ledge cooing a hand's breadth away. She turned from contemplating the view out the window and walked back to where Skänder's secretary was sitting.

'Hi, Saira. How's it going?'

The young woman looked up and smiled, her mouth filled with two even rows of very white teeth. 'Hi, Fran. We haven't seen you for a while. How was the trip?'

'It was really good, thanks. We had a wonderful time.'

'You were in Paris just last week! Oh my God! Where else did you go? You went somewhere pretty weird, didn't you?'

'Tunisia.'

'How was that? Wow! Tunisia! My sister took their two to Disneyland Paris. She said it was just fantastic. Did you guys go there?'

'We didn't go to Disneyland.' Fran felt nauseous. She would have to sit down. The waistband of her skirt was biting into her tummy. She longed to loosen it. It wasn't just gripey guts. She had gripey guts but it wasn't *just* that. Skänder's emails were nuts. He was in a panic about not being ready for the residential short courses for the Chinese executives in September. She felt sick thinking about it. The smell of this building! Why do these new buildings all stink? What is it? The nausea was making it difficult to breathe. She took a slow deep breath of the stale air. Where had it been, for Christ's sake? How many toilets were there on this floor? 'He's expecting me, isn't he?'

'There's someone with him, Fran.' Saira wrinkled her nose. 'He'll buzz in a minute. I'll let him know you're here.' She grimaced. 'You know Carlos.' Carlos, eh! She raised her eyes to the ceiling. They were co-conspirators, after all, weren't they? Us girls. 'Why don't you sit down for a minute. Are you okay? You look a bit pale.'

Fran went over and sat in one of the two red upholstered chairs that stood flanking a low table. International and local education journals neatly fanned on the tabletop. Was that part of Saira's job? To fan out the journals? Fran closed her eyes. She wasn't ready for this.

Saira called, 'He's ready for you, Fran.'

She stood up. She was longing to fart. She held it in with difficulty and smiled at Saira and she went on into Carlos Skänder's enormous office, two sides of which were all window, taking in a grandly important view of the great city of Melbourne. The word was vertiginous. A place from which to take the final leap. Was it great? Come on! Everything Australian is great. The Great Barrier Reef, the Great Australian Bight, the Great Ocean Road, the Great Dividing Range, the Great Sandy Desert. It's all great and none of it is. The smell of the air was different in here. Someone—was it Saira again, doing all these little chores?—had uncorked a pine-scented air freshener, a wick with oriental blooms and a soft light.

Her stomach contracted sharply. Eric Thornton was twisted around in his chair looking at her, his hungry pig eyes running over her, touching her legs, noting the slight bulge of her stomach over the waistband of her skirt. She'd put on three kilos since she'd last worn this skirt, almost five months ago now. He stood up and held out his hand. 'You look fantastic, you know, you really do.'

Thornton's hand was damp. She resisted wiping her palm on her skirt.

Skänder didn't stand up. He looked ill. 'Welcome home, Fran. Eric's right—you look wonderful. White blouses suit you.' He wasn't looking at her. He didn't care. He just wanted the Chinese money. It was supposed to be a Chinese bonanza, wasn't it? The New Gold Mountain, as the Chinese called Australia's goldfields in the nineteenth century. He needed to get in on the act. He had to have his share or fail. Failure might mean suicide. Was there any chance of that? Maybe all these swine would wipe themselves out if the Chinese failed to come through with the money. Mass executive death at the universities. Lemmings pouring over the cliff in a howling torrent of despair. The end of life as we know it. The sun rising on a new world in the morning after the great extinction.

She didn't say, Black makes you look like a fucking undertaker, Eric, but she did think it. She also didn't say, When are you going to die of cancer, you evil runt?

'Sit down. Sit down, Fran. I've asked Eric to join us. I want you to look after him in Hefei and Tianjin. Eric's presence will give the course credibility.'

'I can't believe this!' she said. The shock of it was a fierce jab of contempt in her heart. 'And my presence last year didn't give the course credibility?' Her unsteady breathing betrayed her. 'I've published quite a bit more than Eric, you know.'

Eric Thornton laughed. 'It's true, Carlos.' He gave Fran a special look. Just the two of us in Tianjin, the Chinese moon lighting our way to a night of bliss. You know what I mean, Fran. 'That blouse really does suit you.' He just stopped short of winking. He gave her bare knees a hard, weirdly aggressive look then, as if he might make a lunge and deal with his infected lust then and there.

Fran had crossed her legs automatically when she sat down. She uncrossed them now and gave her hem a tug. His gaze walked all over her, pausing here, moving on, pausing again there, his gaze speaking the unspeakable, the hard edge of his freakish thought making her stomach crawl. She feared him. And she resented her fear, and she caught in his eyes his pleasure at her distress. She felt sick, trapped. Her voice was shaky when she said, 'This is the first I've heard that you want me to go back to China this year, Carlos. You can't just dump it on me like this.'

Carlos Skänder said slowly, making his point as obvious as he could, 'You've been away, Fran. It's been three months. You haven't been responding to my emails. Eric's an AO, Fran. He's on the board of the Australian Academy of the Humanities. The Dawkins Chair of Business Ethics, it's our most prestigious endowed chair. He's performed in his role with great distinction. Okay, so you've published a lot of papers—I know, we all know, and we love you for it, but Fran . . .'

'But I'm not a man? Why don't you just say it, Carlos?'

Skänder sighed and appealed wearily to Eric Thornton. 'Can you give us a minute, Eric?'

'No worries.' Eric Thornton lifted himself out of his chair then turned and placed his briefcase on the seat. He gave Fran a little nod, just between the two of them, and he went out, closing the door of Skänder's office quietly behind him.

Fran realised the death's head portrait of a judge in full ceremonial robes hanging on the wall behind Skänder must be Valerie's father. The small black round eyes of the judge were looking directly at her. She had never really looked at that portrait before. It had always been just another pretentious picture of yet another man of distinction in his robes of office. It was no wonder Valerie's mother suicided! With that thing around the house it was a wonder they hadn't all suicided.

She said, 'I'm not going. I don't feel well. I think I'm going to vomit.'

Carlos Skänder closed his eyes briefly. On the point of anger now, he said, 'Fran, you are going. You will go. The arrangements have been made. You and Eric will be leaving on the first of June. You and I are not going to have another one of our fights over this. This is too important to me, to the university, to the faculty, and to you too. I think you know that if you manage this project successfully for us, I'll be recommending you for a professorship within a year or two. All this fuss and carry-on, it's not sensible of you. Besides, you'll be well treated over there if Eric's with you. His presence will let them know we're serious about this.'

She spoke carefully. 'I was treated with great respect in China last year.' She could stand no more of it. She gave him a bleak stare and stood up.

'What are you doing now?'

'I'm leaving.'

Skänder barked sharply, 'Fran, come back here!'

As she walked across the foyer to the lift she remembered the day she first resisted him. Her heart had pounded and she had been short of breath, and there was that familiar band of tension above her eyes warning of a rise in her blood pressure. She had been told to be careful about it. She experienced it most strongly when she was challenged by one of these bastards in meetings, especially when she had to confront Skänder, knowing he would talk over her, would persist despite her most dedicated resistance—to the point where she had broken into tears and fled the room on that first occasion. Shamed by her weakness, she had forced herself to go back and face him. There was a frozen sense of anticipation when she re-entered the room. Everyone looking at her, waiting for an explosion that didn't come. She had spoken quietly, in a measured tone, and had made her point. The outcome was important to her back then. Now it no longer figured in her calculations. She was done. Skänder staring at her in disbelief that day, his thick purplish lips slightly parted, his shoulders tensed, chubby fingers drumming on the tabletop. But he had remained silent until she finished. Claire caught up with her in the corridor afterwards and said, 'Well done, Fran. You silenced the bastard!' They had laughed, enjoying the little moment of relief and triumph. It was true. She had outfaced Skänder on that occasion and he had been inclined ever since to listen to her before butting in. She had made him feel unsure of what would happen if he were to persist in opposing her beyond a certain point. He knew she would not cringe and lie down but would do something, maybe something dreadful, something that would be out of the ordinary at any rate and would have consequences. Skänder did not like consequences. She had learned that. It was his one weakness. He would still shout her down, but not without a tussle. They had, despite her loathing, gradually formed an understanding, a way of behaving that was not entirely free of her determination and will. The skin across her forehead on that occasion had been so tight with tension she had half-expected something to burst. An artery in her brain. The pressure in there had contained the insane scream that was trying to come out, spittle and sweat and violent movements of her limbs. The chaos remained hidden. Quelled by the force of her will. Did she gain much? She learned something. Something about her own limits she had not been sure of before. Skänder no longer had a free hand. Fuck him! She required him to consider the unforeseen consequences. Well, here was an unforeseen consequence for him to deal with that he would be unlikely to forget.

She remembered with dismay that she had lost Valerie's diary. It was no longer in her bag. She wanted to cry out wildly against them all.

She nodded coldly to Eric Thornton. He was leaning on Saira's desk, harassing her, no doubt—leaning over and trying to get a glimpse of her tits down the front of her dress. She went over to the lifts and pressed the down button. Skänder came out of his office and walked across to her. He stood so close she felt the warmth of his squat body and smelled the garlic on his breath. He said with cold menace in his tone, 'You are going to regret this, Fran.'

The lift doors opened and she stepped into the empty cubicle and touched CAR PARK. She had never felt more certain of anything. She turned around and they looked at each other. She didn't care. Then the doors slid shut. In seven and a half years she would be fifty. On the cusp of being old, as Tom said of himself. She would be a hollow shell by then and would have become one of them, sucked dry by the lack of conscience in this corporate race for Chinese money, or whatever the next thing would be, a grab for power of one kind or another, the vision of education lost long ago.

She was walking across the basement to her car when the enormous fart that had been gathering in her bowels, and which, from having been suppressed, had become a sharp pain in the lower left side of her abdomen, was suddenly available. She stood still and gave it her best. It was richly satisfying to hear the release bellowing for a healthy full three seconds in the weirdly humming silence of that airless place. 'That was the last trumpet,' she said and laughed. She unlocked the Renault and tossed her briefcase onto the passenger seat and took off her overcoat. She stood a moment by the side of the car, raised both arms into the air and closed her eyes and took three deep breaths. She would refuse to be haunted by that horrible look in

Eric Thornton's eyes. But she had seen it, and she knew she was not going to be able to forget it. She had seen that frightening look before, the look that denied her humanity and turned her into a thing to be used. The first time was when she was a schoolgirl and was running for the tram. A man had leaned out of his parked car and grabbed at her, something drooling from his wet lips, the look in his eyes telling her he was in a place beyond normal human reason and would do something awful to her. When she told her mother later, she was crying, the fear coming out of her that she'd been holding on to all day. She had never forgotten the look in that man's eyes. She had seen it again in Eric Thornton's eyes today. He had been getting off on her fear. That was the telling thing. The thing he had not been able to mask. The evil in his mind looking out through his eyes and touching her body. She was vulnerable to that. Naked to it.

She slid into the driver's seat and started the engine. How was she to warn Margie there was this evil in the hearts of some men? Not monsters under her bed, but ordinary men. Men who looked normal and for the most part behaved within the rules of decency. Were even at times gracious. Or would Margie just know it when she met it? Would her instincts protect her? Tragically, not all men were like Margie's dad. Was there any point telling Margie that in the soul of any decent man there was also the soul of a decent woman? The sexes were not so different. It wasn't something she could just *tell* her, though. It was not a plain fact, like being tall or skinny or fat. It was more subtle than that. The evil in them made them cunning. They were masters of disguise and dissimulation. No threat from Skänder could ever make her willingly go to China with Eric Thornton. Or unwillingly. She was not going, and that was that.

She backed out of the parking space, drove to the exit and put her card in the slot, and when the barrier lifted she took the card and drove out into the teeming street. She was losing her silence. It frightened her to know it. If she remained at the university, she would never recover her inner silence. We don't recover something as fundamental to us as that, do we? Expecting to recover it would be like expecting to recover our youth once we are old. If she lost her silence now, she would never have it again, ever. That period of her life, the period when there had still been some hope, would have ended. That was the real price of the professorship Skänder was dangling in front of her. She was no longer mesmerised by that promise. It was futile. She had seen the horror of it. She would lose her ability to dream. Without her silence she would be as lost as Skänder and the others. She would have become one of them. Sanjeev was the only one among them to have kept the silence of his beautiful interior life. It was in his kindly eyes that she saw it. Sanjeev was a man whose soul was intact, like the Berber women. Sanjeev had not joined the ugly ones. He was invisible to them, shielded from the cruelty of their world by his faith, and by their failure to see him. Sanjeev was beyond the limits of their narrow vision. But she possessed no such faith as Sanjeev's, no deep place of belonging to sustain her. She could not be invisible to them. She was not Sanjeev. She was vulnerable and alone. She could not be who she was not. As the Berber woman had said to Valerie's aunt, we can only sing our own song. She, on the other hand, was from a broken people and had lost her song.

* * *

The traffic on the freeway was heavy and fast. While these thoughts of essential silence were going through Fran's mind, great B-doubles weighing hundreds of tonnes thundered past, centimetres from her little yellow Renault. This was not how she was going to die, her broken body trapped in the mangled debris of a collision with one of these monsters on the freeway. How did she know this? She did know it. She just knew. Some things she knew, but didn't know *how* she knew. She would tell Margie, Have sex only when you yourself want to have it. Be the one to choose. Always be the one to decide. Never let them require it from you. It is too private for that. Sex is the most private thing there is. She was not sure how she would actually tell Margie any of this, but surely she would find a way.

She took the off-ramp at Sunbury and headed for the university. She would tell Joseph: Valerie Sommers is still alive! I met her. She's still out there at the judge's house where you worked on the garden with your lovely Mr Cool. The garden is a jungle. I gave her the diary. I had to. She took it. I hated losing it. I'm no longer defended by it. But it was hers. I saw how she wept when she began to read it. It means everything to her. Now it is I who will miss it. She has invited me to call her. She spoke of you with affection. You still mean something kind and good in Valerie Sommers's life, Joseph. She is still your loyal friend. She still believes in you. It was lovely for me to hear this from her. I have not been mistaken about everything, Joseph. You know that. I need you to know it.

Thinking of Joseph, Fran was reassured that Stella Colvin's warning about people didn't apply to everyone. She was not wrong in her admiration for Joseph nor in her deep response to Valerie's diary. They were important to her. They were not her family, they were not her colleagues—indeed, they were people she scarcely knew, but she did know she was not wrong about them. They spoke to her from a world she could put her faith in. Stella might also have said, There are things about some people you'll be glad you know.

* * *

Driving up Jacksons Hill past the new housing, the rows of naked little villa units with their tiny patches of fake grass outside looked like so many cells in a camp for refugees, temporary residents who must be ready to move on at a moment's notice when the extension of the visa was denied. There was nothing permanent about them. Fran saw *through* them to the familiar paddock they had been built on. She remembered the paddock with frost on the grass in the morning.

Towards the crest of the hill a large sign blocked off half the road: DANGER: CONSTRUCTION SITE. She drove carefully around the sign. The car park in front of the main building was fenced off with orange safety netting, the plastic strips shuddering in the breeze. A young woman wearing a vibrant yellow jacket several sizes too large for her stood at the top of the driveway holding a red stop sign. The young woman's hands were lost in the sleeves of the dazzling yellow jacket. Trucks and four-by-four twin cabs of the tradies were parked within the taped-off area. There was a continuous chorus of high-pitched beeping from vehicles and various pieces of equipment that were reversing then going forward again. Fran was pulled up by the young woman, who thrust the sign at her and shook it. She had to wait while a long truck with an even longer trailer

manoeuvred on the roadway ahead of her. Fran lowered her
window and asked the woman, 'So what's going on?'

The woman turned and greeted her cheerfully, as if all
this was an elaborate new game that was being set up. She
bent down to Fran's window and pointed off to the left. 'The
temporary car park's down there. Just follow the signs when
this bloke's made his turn.'

Fran parked her car and went back and walked in through
the main entrance and went into Skänder's office. She shut the
door behind her and put on the light. The office was cold
and still, invaded by noise and disuse, the forlorn emptiness of
it. She stood looking at the portrait behind his desk. A brass
plaque attached to the bottom of the gilt frame gave the names
of the subject and the artist: *Portrait of Valerie Sommers*. The
name of the artist was Josephine Muntz-Adams. Fran had never
heard of her. There was a date next to the black signature on
the bottom left of the painting. She leaned close but couldn't
decipher it.

There she was, the so-called 'troubled' twenty-one-year-old,
bewitched by the life of the women in the bey's old mansion
in Sidi Bou Said. The *mad* woman who had lived for five years in
Fran's office, a patient in the mental hospital. There was nothing
in this portrait to suggest a likeness to the old woman Fran
had met at the judge's house. Here was a young woman with

smooth, full cheeks, a private amusement in her large dark eyes, looking off somewhere beyond the picture plane, and maybe thinking of the rainbow lorikeets eating the director's apples, or of her lover, Jessie. But of course, Fran reminded herself, this portrait was painted before her life at the asylum. There were no signs of sufferings past or to come in the eyes of this young woman. Her dark hair was short and smart, shaped by a professional into the simple style of the day. She was wearing a cream open-necked shirt and a dark tweed jacket with lapels. Her expression was not that of a troubled soul, but was calm, even contemplative. Her lips, which were catching the light, were soft and full. Was she beautiful? She was interesting. Intelligent, thoughtful, considering something in her own mind rather than impressed with the situation of the portrait and the artist who was studying her. Yes, Fran decided, this young woman possessed an unusual beauty of her own; she was not a make-believe person, not being someone else, not making herself up—indeed, not wearing make-up. Before this, Fran had not taken any notice of the portrait, but here was the likeness of a woman whom she would remember. She already knew her. Fran was confident she was looking at the young woman who had written the poem 'Jessie'. She spoke aloud the words of the first verse: *'Am I not her love? / Her valiant saluki? / Her hound of heaven? / My gaze that of a poet dreaming / Of hunting with my mistress.'* Would she ever find her own self within that private world of Valerie's poem? She had entered the likeness of it for a blessed moment in Hefei. Wasn't that its likeness? That enchanted night, that other world which seemed to her now a fairy tale that someone she trusted had once told her. A place that existed somewhere in memory. She closed her eyes and tried to think of him, to give substance to her thought of him lying with her, to find the presence of his being within herself so that she might set it against the realities of her life. The noise of the trucks and machines outside the window invaded her head. She opened her eyes. It was no good. The university had its own pervasive smell. Hard, old and decayed.

Valerie had known herself. Like Sanjeev, like Joseph, Valerie, this young woman of the portrait, the young woman of the poem, had known who she was. There was no doubt of that. These people knew who they were. Hadn't she sung her own song and been wounded for it by the Skänders and their power? Wasn't that it? The dead people had done their best to destroy her.

Fran came out of Skänder's office and was hit by the blast of noise. She closed his door and crossed the foyer and went around the back of the staircase. The door to the cloisters was propped open. The sun had come out and was shining on the courtyard. Two workmen wearing kneepads were kneeling on the cobbles. They had lifted a wide area of the old uneven cobbled surface and were tapping the cobblestones down into a newly prepared base of clean yellow sand. Their tapping was noiseless. They were using black rubber hammers. Fran stopped to watch them, then hurried on to the end of the cloisters. She had never visited the cloisters in the daylight before. Was this really the same place she had been with Joseph that dark rainy night?

The door to Joseph and Eleni's apartment had been taken off its hinges and was leaning against the wall. She stood at the threshold looking in. The homely living room she remembered no longer existed. The room was empty, cold, bare. Even the old iron fireplace in which Joseph and Eleni had had a wood fire burning that night had been removed and set to one side, the chimney space like a wide open mouth, black, empty of teeth. The internal wall to the right of the doorway where Fran was standing had been partially removed and the floorboards lifted. Two tradesmen were laying service cables in the space under the floor. There was a nose-tingling smell of freshly disturbed plaster dust in the air. Fran called, 'Hello there.'

The younger of the two men looked up. His gaze went over her, checking her out. 'G'day,' he said. 'How's it goin'?'

'Where are Joseph and Eleni? The couple who lived here?'

The young man looked at the older man. 'You'll have to ask the people at the uni.' The older man didn't look around or pause in his work. The younger one smiled at her.

She went out and walked back through the cloisters and into the foyer, then continued on into the car park and crossed to the old infirmary building. She was hurrying now, a feeling of panic barely held at bay, acting normally in a situation that was no longer normal.

The facility manager's office was on the ground floor of the old infirmary. Nadia Petrovic was sitting behind her desk. There was a bunch of yellow daisies in a glass jug beside her computer. The sun was shining through her window, the noise of the activity outside was pleasantly muted, the office bright, the air fresh, Nadia herself shiny and clean, even radiant, a devotee of the gym, her lovely face made up with great care, subtle, tinted. Her desk tidy and bare. The first of her family to graduate from university, Nadia Petrovic looked to Fran to be scarcely more than twenty years of age.

Nadia looked up from her screen and smiled. 'Hi, Fran! So you guys are back! Did you have a wonderful time?'

'Where's Joseph, Nadia?'

'Joseph?'

'Where is he?'

Nadia made an exaggerated grief face. 'Oh, you haven't heard?'

A chilling shot of adrenaline hit Fran's bladder and she gave a sharp little cry. *Please don't tell me!* She didn't speak, but her lips moved.

'Oh, Fran! His wife passed. Were you a friend? I'm so sorry to be the bearer of bad news.'

'So where's Joseph gone?'

Nadia's grief mask modified into a mournful expression, which brightened after two seconds into a look of relief and delight—problem solved! 'The university had to let him go. We've outsourced the caretaker's responsibilities to a Melbourne firm. They're good. I believe Joseph is happy with his new apartment. Very happy.' She paused. 'Would you like me to make you a coffee, Fran?'

'No, thanks.'

'The dean's putting pressure on the tradies to get the cloister apartments ready for the Chinese executives. We're expecting them in September. It's exciting, isn't it? There are some great fittings going in. You should see them! It's brought this dull old place alive, I can tell you. It makes coming in to work a pure joy.'

Pure joy.

She drove slowly, hoping to spot Joseph's ute. There was no sign of the ute, but it was obvious the row of yellow-brick villa units behind the railway station car park at the bottom of Jacksons Hill was the new development Nadia had told her to look for. She read the sign out the front: SUNRISE CRESCENT GARDENS. Each unit was offset at a slight angle from its neighbour, a coffin-sized patch of fake grass out the front. She pulled in off the road and parked outside number nine. It was the closest unit to the road. Cars and trucks and SUVs roaring past on the road. She stepped out of the Renault. A gilded plastic horseshoe knocker and a spy-hole in the centre of the front door, an outsize black 9 on a white square on the wall next to it.

Jenny was barking even before Fran knocked. Joseph opened the door at once. Fran scarcely recognised him. He looked crumpled, ten years older than the upright man she had last seen before Christmas. In the four months since then Joseph had become an old man. He stared at her, his expression anguished. The little white dog was eagerly jumping up at Fran.

Joseph said, 'I thought you were the ranger.' He looked out into the road, nervous and distracted, then leaned down and drew Jenny inside. 'They won't let me keep her here.'

Fran stepped into the room and Joseph closed the door. 'Who won't let you keep her? Where's your ute?'

Joseph was rummaging among a mess of papers on the small square table she had last seen in the cloister apartment, searching helplessly for something. He was obviously in a state of panic and spoke in a nervous rush, no longer the composed Joseph she had known, a quiet man then whose confidence she had trusted, a man who had surely owned his silence. She saw how afraid and lost he had become, how fragile and tormented. She had been expecting him to steady her.

'Dogs aren't allowed,' he said. 'I'm the only one renting. They all own their own villas. You can have one cat. Eleni's cat had to be put down. I don't have a say. They have a committee. The chairwoman of the committee has a cat. I have a letter from her here. It's signed by her. I'll show you. The ranger is coming today. I was going to take Jenny with me and run away. I thought you were him coming to get her.'

Fran stepped up to him and put her arm around his shoulders. 'Joseph!'

He stopped rummaging and looked at her.

'You can't stay here. All right? You just can't. It's too awful. I won't let you. We have a cottage on the farm. It needs some work, but it's fine. It's mostly restored. There's a fireplace. You can come out to the farm and stay in the cottage till we find you somewhere decent to live.'

The noise of the trucks accelerating away from the traffic lights by the station twenty metres from the front door was deafening. She had to wait until the worst of it had passed. In the tiny room with its single window she felt as if there was scarcely space to breathe. The only furniture was Eleni and Joseph's armchairs from the cloisters, Eleni's chair facing the wall, cardboard cartons here and there about the floor, the tiny kitchenette bench with a microwave oven, and this table. On the floor, lying on its back, the red cedar corner cupboard from Valerie's cell.

'They've sent for the ranger,' he said. 'He's going to take Jenny to the pound. I don't know what to do.'

Fran said, 'I'm so sorry about Eleni.'

'She would have called me a fool.'

She thought he was going to weep. She said, 'I'll take Jenny home with me this afternoon. All right? Tom will bring his ute and pick you up with your things tomorrow and bring you out to the farm. He'll go with you to the agent to get your contract cancelled. They're sure to make a fuss about your bond. Tom's good at dealing with that sort of thing. He's gracious and patient and it works for him. If it was me, I'd lose my temper with them and we'd get nowhere. After tonight you won't need to stay here another night.'

'I've never lived anywhere except up the hill there.' He pulled a handkerchief out of his overall pocket and blew his nose vigorously, wiping and blowing and wiping then blowing again. He stuffed the handkerchief back into the breast pocket of his overalls and looked squarely at Fran.

She said, 'I'll make us a cup of tea. Everything's going to be okay.' He needed her. She would help him. His frailty made her feel strong and capable. He had steadied her after all, but not as she had expected. She had thought he would be the strong one.

He said, 'Thank you for coming to see me, Dr Egan.'

She took his arm. 'Show me where your tea things are. What happened to your ute?'

'The ute wasn't mine. The ute is university property.'

Jenny made a rush at the door, barking frantically. There were three loud knocks. Joseph flinched.

Fran said, 'Let me get it.'

Joseph picked up Jenny and held her in his arms. Fran went over and opened the door.

A young woman in clean, neatly pressed green overalls with an official insignia on the breast pocket stood there, alert and ready for action.

Fran said, 'You're the ranger?'

'Yes. Sorry. I've come to get the dog. Sorry.' She leaned to one side in an effort to see around Fran to where Joseph was cradling Jenny in his arms.

'The dog's mine,' Fran said. 'Mr Bayer has been looking after her while we've been overseas. I've come to take her home with me. I'm afraid they've sent you out on a wild-goose chase.'

The young woman said, 'Is the dog registered?'

'The dog? Her name's Jenny. She'll be with me out on the farm in a couple of hours. If you need to make further enquiries you can come out and see us there. Thank you.' Fran smiled and closed the door firmly, then stood looking through the spy-hole. After half a minute she turned around and grinned at Joseph. 'Gone! We shan't see her again. Let's have that cup of tea.'

* * *

They were sitting facing each other: Fran on Eleni's old chair and Joseph on his own chair. Jenny was lying on the rug that had been in front of the fireplace in Joseph and Eleni's apartment. Her old rag rug. Joseph was smoking a cigarette, his mug of tea beside his chair on the floor. He had been describing how Eleni had gone downhill quickly, not long after Fran's visit. He was looking at Jenny. He leaned down and picked up his mug and took a drink of tea and put the mug down on the floor again.

They sat for some minutes, neither speaking, the intermittent roar of the traffic broken by brief intervals of quiet.

'Eleni was out for a walk,' Joseph said during a moment of silence. 'She was in a supervised group in the garden.'

Fran was relieved to see that some of the colour had come back into his cheeks and he was a lot calmer.

'When the weather was fine they let a few well-behaved patients from the locked ward out for a supervised walk in the gardens once a week. They were given this walk out in the fresh air as a special reward. Not all of them were offered the privilege. They had to behave. It didn't happen every week, only now and then. I was weeding or planting flowers. I don't remember for sure what I was doing. It was Eleni's first time on the supervised walk. I had never seen her before. I stood up and she was looking at me. She smiled and said, "We need the butterflies." I knew in that moment that I had met my life's companion. The sound of her voice enchanted me. I said to her—just to keep the conversation going, you know—"Any particular kind of butterflies?" The locked ward patients weren't allowed to speak to anyone. Some of them got upset easily and became difficult. You only had to say hello to some of them and they were off. When the group walked past me, Eleni turned and looked back and said, "The ones in your belly, Joseph." I was astonished that she knew my name! "When you're going to do something that scares you but you know you're going to do it anyway," she said. And the way she laughed then. Her courage and her beauty were shining just for me. Joseph, she had said, the butterflies in your belly.

'I looked out for her after that and when I saw her again she stepped out of line for me and we held hands, as if we had both understood. That caused us a lot of trouble. The supervisors didn't like anyone stepping out of line. They were afraid it would catch on and the whole thing would come undone, crazy people going in all directions. They were afraid they would lose control, so they overreacted and started screaming at everyone to get back in the line. The supervisors became the scary ones. But they didn't scare her. From the first moment of our first meeting, and her telling me we needed the butterflies, we both knew we had each other, and that was that. We laughed. The whole line had to halt and stand still on the path and wait. The supervisor came up to us to get her back into line and Eleni tightened her grip on my hand. And I tightened my grip on her hand too. We understood this was the big test for us. They would have to tear us apart.

'She never did get back into line. We stood up to them. She said to the supervisor, not yelling and screaming but saying it quietly, just for him to hear, as if she really did have the power to defy him, "I'm not on my own now, Mr Stone." That was his name: Stone. Some people always have the right name. They had other names for him, but Stone was the right one. She told me most of the patients were terrified of him. He had power over the women in the locked ward. Now he didn't know what to do. Eleni held on to me and I held on to her. I was in love. He asked me, "Will you please let her go, Joseph?" I said, "No, I will never let her go." And I smiled at him. "And you cannot make me let her go."

'Standing there facing down Mr Stone was the best moment of my life. I vowed to myself that no matter what happened, Eleni would always be able to count on me standing by her. Knowing this made me feel my own strength in a way I had never felt it before. I remember I thought to myself, with great surprise, Maybe I am a man of courage after all. I felt like laughing. I knew my will was stronger than Mr Stone.

'I liked Eleni's accent too. It was another thing about her. I said to her, "Where are you from?" She said, "I am a Greek." I said, "A Greek goddess." She said, "Yes, just what you've been dreaming of. And where do you come from?" So I told her, "I came here with my mother from Poland after the war."'

He looked at Fran. 'Eleni and I wouldn't have made it if it hadn't been for Mr and Mrs Cool. The director, old

Vincent-Sinclair, was fond of Mr Cool and saw how being in love with me had steadied Eleni and was going to be the making of me. Mr Cool asked the director to help us. Vincent-Sinclair stepped in and sorted things out for us. We were married in the asylum chapel.

'Eleni was a woman who had passion in her soul. Passion for everything she did. She had fought the cruel baiting of the voices since she was a teenager all on her own, alone until I met her, and those voices were often beating her down. She was afraid of them but she fought back like crazy. Sometimes the voices won and she had to crawl into a corner and howl, which was why she was in the hospital. When the voices were in charge they took over everything. It was a torment for her. Sometimes she broke things that people valued, just to get the voices out. They required sacrifices from her. It was the only thing that would make them shut up. At those times they had to restrain her. She told me she had done quite a lot of damage. After, I joined her in the battle against the voices, and she could reach for my hand whenever they threatened to control her. Together we drove the voices into a corner like a bunch of wild things and penned them there. They frightened us but we found the courage and stood up to them. Like bullies, they couldn't stand being defied. We imagined a special room for the voices and only we had the key to that room. We had them cornered and they knew it. We had a locked ward for them. They were still with her at the end, you know. They never died. The voices are immortal. You can't kill them. They never completely went away. Even when they were quiet, you could feel them stirring, black and restless and likely to rise up and start their ranting. At the end, when she was weak and wanted to give up, they came back and began to bully her again. The voices were relentless. And that is what they were: bullies.

'That night you came to see us, the night I gave you Valerie Sommers's diary, Eleni was not well. She was vulnerable and the voices came and tormented her. That night was the first time ever that Eleni and I were defeated by them. I had no power over them without her will to hold my hand and join our power against them. She howled that night. She was insane. Yes, that is the word for it. She was in torment. There was nothing I could do. They told her to kill herself and she gave in and just wanted to do it. The drugs put her to sleep for an hour and I had some peace before the nightmare started up again.' He was silent a while, then he looked at Fran and he said, 'She is gone.'

Fran was moved and had nothing to say. Joseph smoked his cigarette and watched Jenny. The little dog was quivering in her sleep.

Fran said, 'I met Valerie Sommers. She is still living at her old family home.'

He looked at her, coming back from the distance of his thoughts. 'Valerie Sommers?'

'I went to look at the old house. I didn't expect to meet her, of course; I thought she was dead. But she was there. She still lives there. She is old and frail, but she is still spirited. It was hard to believe she was the same person who wrote the diary. She asked me why I had come and I showed her the diary and told her how you had rescued it and given it to me. She wept when she saw it. I think it is all she has left. You have given her back her reason to hope, Joseph. When I told her it was you who rescued it from the workmen, she was moved. She remembers you with sincere friendship and would love to see you again. She asked me to call her. Perhaps you and I will be able to go and see her together one of these days?'

Joseph was thoughtful. He did not respond to her suggestion. Eventually he said, 'If you take Jenny to your farm, I'll be here on my own.'

'It will only be for one night.'

He looked up at Fran. 'Jenny and I are all that's left of it, Dr Egan.'

She could think of nothing to say to this. An old man and his little white terrier, chance survivors marooned on this tiny island in the middle of the roar and rumble of the traffic. They did not belong here. No one belonged here. No one belongs in this present world. None of us. We've created a hell for ourselves out of the Paradise of our dreams. The so-called villa trembled when the big rigs went by, their powerful engines accelerating through the gears. The noise was painful. It wasn't a haven the university had found for him but a prison. Inside, Joseph was trapped; outside, and without a vehicle of his own, he was lost.

He said, 'To be without her, even for a night . . .' He shook his head and did not finish his thought.

Fran said, 'The night will pass and tomorrow will come and so will Tom. And you and Jenny will be reunited.'

Joseph said, 'And what about if she doesn't want to go with you?'

'Why don't we ask her and see?'

Joseph said to Jenny, 'Would you like to go with Dr Egan to her farm?'

Jenny raised her head and looked at Joseph.

Fran stood up. 'I'll go and sit in the car and leave the passenger-side door open. Okay?'

Jenny got up and ran to the door ahead of her.

Fran went out and got in the car. She was worried that she was doing the wrong thing. Joseph was looking anxious and downcast. Jenny was standing in the doorway looking across at the car. She was alert and trembling with anticipation. Joseph stood behind her. He said unhappily, 'Well, you know, you can go with Dr Egan if you want to.'

Jenny sprinted up to the car and leaped in with one bound. She sat up on the passenger seat, looking straight ahead through the windscreen, ready.

Fran saw a smile sneak into Joseph's expression. She breathed a sigh of relief. It was amazing to see the change the smile brought to him. He appeared to shed those dark ten years that had grown on him while she was away, and something of the calm Joseph she had known was there.

He walked across to the car and leaned down and looked in at her. 'Dogs are brighter than people. Thank you for doing this, Dr Egan. I was at a loss when you turned up. I did not know what I was going to do. What time can I expect to see Mr Egan in the morning? I'll have everything ready for him.'

Jenny ignored him, trembling, tense in case the excursion was called off.

The downs—you could only call them that—went on forever, the soft rises and slopes undulating like the body of some great bloated beast, replete, full, a warm and friendly landscape of sunlight and shadow. Crowds of people, hundreds of them, some scattered about, many in close groups at what seemed to be selected areas, where the events, she understood, would soon take place. She had been told it was an annual fair, a public holiday of some kind held on the same day each year, an old tradition. And wasn't she in Somerset? Tom's mother's home? Indeed, Tom's childhood home. The weather was fine and sunny and the people were all with their families, young couples with children. She noticed she was the only one who was on her own. She examined sections of the crowd, but she couldn't see anyone else on their own, and no old people, no grannies or grandads. Everyone was of early child-rearing age, the oldest of them in their mid-forties, most still in their twenties and thirties. Fit, healthy, happy and young. Out there on the downs celebrating life. The children were also young, maybe eight or ten at the oldest. Mostly, however, the children were still toddlers staggering about the place testing their steps, closely attended by awed dads and mums. They were all happy. Every one of them. No tantrums. Fran knew herself to be an outsider. An intruder even. No one looked sideways at her. The events hadn't begun yet.

She hadn't seen him, but Tom must be around somewhere. She would run into him in a minute. They had arranged to meet here. She had not expected there to be so many people. She had expected to see him sitting on a bench or under a tree waiting for her, more or less on his own. But come to think of it, she noticed now, there were no benches and no trees. Nowhere to sit really unless you sat on the ground. But no one was sitting on the ground. The open downs were unfenced and treeless to the horizon. She had not expected Somerset to look like this. There was a strangeness and she had begun to feel uneasy. Maybe it was being a bit older than most of them and the only one who was alone that was making her uneasy, giving her this feeling that she was not in the right place. That she had turned up at the wrong place, losing her way somehow. When had she lost her way? What if she were to backtrack? Perhaps, after all, this was not where she was supposed to be?

And where was Tom? She stood and looked about. Where *was* he? With Tom by her side she would be restored. It was an odd word to use, but she meant restored to being one half of a couple, like all the others. And the kids were with him, weren't they? She knew they were. Then they would be a proper family again. Weren't the kids with him? Thinking about it now, she did begin to wonder if Margie and Tommy were with him or were somewhere else. Sleeping over with friends maybe? But Tommy didn't really have friends, did he? Except for Ina. He and Ina were friends. So he said.

She couldn't remember the exact arrangement they had made, nor where they were when they had arranged to meet here. Why couldn't she remember? Maybe the kids were at school. But surely not here? This was not Australia. This was not *home*.

The fear just came to her; suddenly it was there. She did not know why she was afraid. What was she afraid of? Everything was so beautiful and perfect. There was something she had not understood, something that all these other happy couples *had* understood.

She decided to get away from the open downs and find a normal street with shops and ordinary people, where she could be confident of finding Tom waiting for her, being patient and normal and probably interested in something he'd found in a shop window. She could picture him. Standing there gazing in at a collection of old tools that had belonged to his grandfather. She would walk up to him and take his arm and say, 'Sorry, darling! I got a bit lost back there on the open downs. It was all just too much.' And they would go on together arm in arm, just like everyone else, and maybe find a nice cafe where they could have lunch and talk about the thing in the shop window that had interested him. A gadget, or some old cabinet-maker's hand tool. Just a nice quiet moment on their own away from the crowds on the downs. Nothing important.

She found a street in the end. The street she found was busy with traffic and people. It was reassuringly normal. It was not too crowded. All the shops were open and busy serving customers. She felt relieved to have got away from the wide open spaces out there. It had felt lonely and unnatural, threatening even. She looked at the people who were gazing in shop windows but couldn't see him. In fact, she noticed that once again there were no single people, only couples. But no children. This whole thing was surely some kind of trap that had been prepared for her and she was walking straight into it. She knew then she wasn't going to find Tom again. Ever! It hit her like the crack of doom (another of her mother's old sayings). The conviction that she had lost Tom surged through her, knocking her sideways. She knew what it was. It was clear. It was a family open day and she was alone forever. With despair in her heart, she said aloud, 'Oh, God! I've lost Tom!'

* * *

She woke to the sound of her own voice. *Tom*, she had said. Her anchor to normality. Not the children. It was still daylight. Early evening. She could hear herself saying, I've lost Tom, in that stricken voice. An echo of it. Like an afterimage on the retina, fading in her brain. The last of the low sun was shining through the window across the room onto the far wall. She was fully dressed. The light cotton throw rug was over her legs. Tom must have come in and put it there. She knew at once it had been a dream of loss and guilt. Its title, *Family Open Day*, was in her mind. Open day on the open downs. She saw its meaning at once and laughed. It was not a happy laugh. She could still hear herself saying, I've lost Tom, faint now. But still troubling. The real voices she could hear were on the radio in the kitchen. The slam of the flywire door. Margie was whistling. Going out to pen up the chooks so the fox wouldn't get them. Fran lay there piecing together her reality. Her day. It was still the same day. Skänder's sinister warning as she waited for the lift doors to open and admit her. For an instant she thought her fear in the dream had been fear of Skänder, of what he might do. But of course Skänder had nothing to do with it.

Family Open Day! How open with her family was she supposed to be? She saw, with the clearest thought it is possible to have, looking straight down through to the bottom of the thing, to the limpid source of it, that she and her lover had been just two human beings who had met and created between them a little moment of ecstasy. That was all. Innocent. A gift. Leave it alone. Its purity was sacrosanct. Were they not also simply children of this world themselves? Passing through. Human beings. Here one moment, gone the next. Like the stricken voice of her dream, she realised that her special night in the hotel room with him in far-off Hefei was withdrawing into the past like the bright trail of a comet that will pass only once in every ten thousand years, leaving its indelible effects behind in the dreams and fears of the people who had witnessed it. The ripples in the stream of life. Nothing could be done about them. She could no longer grasp the clarity of it. Soon it would be gone. Her sadness was greater than her fear now.

It was all so sad. Then she remembered Jenny and swung her legs off the bed and stood up. The wave of dizziness made her reach for the back of the chair that stood by the door. She steadied herself and looked down at the rumpled bedclothes. Looking down at the bedclothes made her think of the knowing male child she had given birth to, an alien creature that knew everything about her. Her ageless conscience, she supposed it was. Her fear that her lover had made her pregnant. The knowing infant she had given birth to in her dream was not even a toddler. A fierce little thing that saw the two of them in the hotel room in Hefei that night as filthy cheats, traitors to the sacred family group. Evil outsiders. Was she? Was that what she really was, if only she could face the truth of it? Family Open Day: a nightmare, not a dream. She had to sit down on the edge of the bed for a minute and think.

So, had it been a dream of memory and guilt? But not remorse? She refused to feel remorse. She would burn at the stake before she repudiated him and their sacred night in Hefei. Sacred? The piercing clarity of it might be fading into the past, but it was still beautiful and true, and it was hers. How was she to get rid of that image of the knowing child? She stood up again and went out into the kitchen. There was no one about. The outside light was on over at the dairy. Tom must be in his workshop. She turned around and went to Tommy's room. She knocked gently then opened the door. Tommy was sitting at his desk with his back to her, bending over his writing; he wrote longhand in a notebook with a pen, scorning the laptop that all the other kids used. He looked around at her. Jenny was lying in a warm hollow on his bed. The little dog raised its head.

Fran said, 'Hello, darling. Jenny looks as if she's at home with you.'

Tommy said, 'She's my new friend. Are you all right, Mum?'

'I'm fine, darling. Why?' She ran her hands through her hair. 'I must look a fright. I needed a lie-down. Where's your dad?'

'Can we keep her?'

'Jenny is Joseph's. He'll be coming out to stay in the cottage for a little while. Till we can find them both somewhere decent to live.'

'Why can't they just stay in the cottage forever? We don't need the cottage, do we?'

'We'll see.'

* * *

The four of them sitting up at the table in the kitchen eating the spanakopita Tom had made earlier in the day. They had green tomato chutney with it. Another of Tom's recipes for using up garden produce at the end of the season, tomatoes that weren't going to ripen and would only rot if he left them on the bush. He had fried the potatoes in butter and cooked broad beans from the garden. He was drinking beer. Fran stuck with the red wine. Margie was silent. They were all silent, attending to their food. The silence was unusual at the table and was largely due to the fact that Margie had just told them she wanted to go back to England to live with her grannie in Somerset. Tom and Fran had not said anything to this yet. Tommy was trying to get

Jenny to eat a pinch of his spanakopita, but Jenny seemed to think it was a game and not real food.

Tom said, 'I've run an extension lead down to the cottage for Joseph.'

'That's good.'

'I lit a fire in the big room and put in a stock of wood. We should keep it going all night. It will drive out the damp.'

'What's he going to sleep on?'

'Your dad's old camp bed. I gave it a good clean. It's still in perfect nick.'

Margie said, 'Aren't either of you going to say anything about me going back to live with Grannie?'

Tom and Fran looked at each other. While they were visiting Tom's mother over Christmas, Margie had made friends with one of the boys from the village. A tall, pale, strong lad, with a quiet manner and deep amber eyes that made you want to look at him, and when you did look at him you saw that he was engaged in some deep and elaborate calculation. Fran had found him attractive but slightly odd. He worried her. He was seventeen, three years older than Margie, and owned a motorbike. He was polite and reserved and tended to stand back and listen. He seemed to earn a living doing odd jobs. Tom liked him and was glad to see Margie getting on so well with a local. The boy's name was William. And when Tom said, 'Will might have been me thirty years ago,' Margie told him William didn't like being called Will or Bill. 'His name is William.' He came to dinner. Tom's mother had known him since he was born. He had a sister and an older brother who had both gone to live in London. Tom's mother and William were friends. There was a small apple orchard behind Tom's mother's cottage with a bench seat and a view across to the Quantock Hills, and a long patch of rising ground where she grew her vegetables. William mowed the grass for her and weeded. From the bench in the orchard, William told them, they might see the stag hunters riding by across the ridges some mornings and hear the huntsman's horn. Fran said she feared for the poor deer they would pull down with those dogs. William said respectfully, 'It is indeed a melancholy affair.' And Margie said loftily, 'You don't understand, Mum.' And Fran said, 'And you do?' And then there was an awkward silence. William's phrase stayed with her, neither celebrating the hunt nor condemning it, seeing in it something venerable, something antique, almost a part of nature itself. It might have been the waning of the moon that he referred to. Would he love Margie? Would she love him? Would they enjoy together that brief moment of having toddlers running about the place on the open downs? She could not imagine it. She feared the worst for Margie.

She said, 'You need to finish your schooling here, darling. You can always go over and stay with Grannie for some of your gap year.'

Margie looked at Tom. 'Dad, say something.'

Tom took a drink of beer and set the stubby down and cleared his throat. 'Well, you know, you're fourteen. I was only just fifteen when I left home and came to Australia on my own.' He looked at Fran and smiled. 'It worked out for us.'

Fran said impatiently, 'It's hardly the same thing.'

'No, that's true. But then nothing ever is. The same thing, I mean. I had no one here. Not a soul. Margie would have Mum and a nice home to go to.' He looked at Margie. 'Did you talk about it with Grannie?'

'It was partly her idea. She said she would love it if I came to stay with her. She said she would pay for my fees at a private school in Taunton. But I had to talk to you guys first.'

Fran took a drink of wine and set the glass down and she breathed. She was thinking of the awful email from Skänder. She had known she shouldn't look at her emails before dinner, but she had looked anyway. Margie had Tom on her side. Fran probably wouldn't have objected to the idea if it had not been for the strange boy, William. She felt him waiting there silently for Margie to come back without her parents. Yes, he was strange. Not bad or evil or anything like that, but strange. Foreign. That phrase, the melancholy of the hunt. It belonged to an older person. Had he read it somewhere? Was he trying to impress them? That village in winter. A picture on a calendar. But she would hate to live there. So tight and enclosed and everyone knowing everyone else. And then this oddness that she couldn't place. The village street empty and silent so much of the time. What were people thinking? What were they doing inside their cottages? Margie had stayed with Tom at his mother's place while she and Tommy went to Tunisia and visited Sidi Bou Said. William had not been in the picture then. He was there when they got back. Tommy kept aloof and watched on. She hadn't asked him what he thought of William. She hadn't needed to.

She said, 'Finish year ten next year. We can talk about it again if you still want to go. You're too young now.'

Tom said, 'I don't think that's quite fair, darling. There are students Margie's age who go on exchange to France and Germany and the States without really knowing the people they're going to be staying with. It's what they do these days. It's broadening. You're the educator—you should be all for it.'

'Well, I'm not all for it. And they don't go on exchange at fourteen. Let's forget it for the moment. I find it hard to put my mind to it.'

Tommy left the table and Jenny trotted along with him.

Fran watched him leave. 'That little dog's adopted him. What's Joseph going to think?'

Tom said, 'You're not being fair to Margie. We have to take her wishes seriously.'

Margie murmured, 'Thanks, Dad.'

Fran said, 'Does that boy William have anything to do with this?'

Margie said angrily, 'Mum! Dad, tell her to shut up.'

Tom said, 'We should be able to do this and stay civilised about it.' He sounded a bit sad. Margie was about to get up. He put his hand on her hand. 'Just let's deal with it. It's not such a difficult thing that we can't deal with it.'

Fran refilled her wineglass and took a sip.

Tom gave her a long look.

'What?' she said. 'Are you saying it's me?'

Margie said, 'It *is* you. It's all right when it's something *you* care about, but when it's one of us you don't care.'

Tom said, 'Why don't we just take a step back for a minute.'

Fran laughed. 'You're so fucking irritating when you're being reasonable. For Christ's sake, get upset for a change. Doesn't anything shift you out of your groove?'

'I'm in a groove?'

'You've always been in a groove.'

Tom said, 'Don't try to make out this is about you and me. This is about Margie.'

Fran said, 'Being about Margie is being about us.'

Margie kicked her chair back and stood up and made a choking sound and went to her room and slammed the door so hard the walls trembled.

There was a long silence, then Fran said, 'I suppose all this is normal.'

'You shouldn't have done that.'

'I know. I'm a bitch. The dean told me that today too.'

'You're not a bitch. But you are a bit unfair to Margie sometimes.'

'I don't think that boy's right for her. He seemed a bit odd. Bewitched.' She laughed.

'William? Is this really about William for you? Mum will take care of her. She'll be as safe there as she is here. Safer.'

'Yes, clutching on to him on his motorbike out on the moor. How safe can a young girl get?'

'She's a young woman. She's going to have relationships with boys whether you're nice about it or not. You can alienate her this way, you know. It's not difficult.'

'The thing is, we're always at each stage of our life only once, and for the first and last time. We don't get to rethink our decisions. We don't get a chance to learn how to do the right thing when we fuck up the first time. That's it. One go. Then it's the next stage of life and we're wondering how the fuck to react to this new thing. Then it's done and it's something else.' She drank the wine and refilled her glass and stood up.

Tom said, 'Don't just leave the table. You're belting the wine down.'

'Oh, shut up, for God's sake.' She said this in a quietly resigned tone of voice. She went into the living room and opened the Ned Kelly and poked the fire into life and put in a couple of pieces of wood. She sat on the sofa and picked up her wine and drank some of it and stared emptily into the fire. Then she closed her eyes. Just to make sense of it all would be good. She had abandoned her career, betrayed her husband, alienated her daughter, given back the diary, that little saviour of a book. What else? Surely that wasn't all? She had fucked up. She was angry. All those happy young people in the dream of the open downs. Open Family Day. She opened her eyes. She put her glass down on the coffee table. She would go and talk to Margie.

She didn't move. Tom was clearing away the dinner things. If he started humming some tuneless thing she would kill him. Seriously. This is where I live. This is who I am. I need help. She would call Valerie in the morning and go and see her. It wouldn't matter if they just sat in silence for an hour and said absolutely nothing. She tried to remember the opening lines of the poem for Jessie but couldn't. Her brain had shut that door. There is no escape from being me, here, now. She reached for the glass and drank the rest of the wine. She knew it wouldn't help. She knew it would make things worse. She cared. She didn't care. Tom was humming behind his mask of tonelessness.

If only she could believe in God. Joseph would be here in the morning. Joseph and his dog. What was she going to do? She could pretend to be having a breakdown. But surely anyone who pretends to be having a breakdown is having a breakdown, aren't they? Isn't that a symptom? What do the psychiatrists say? Go ahead, Dr Egan! Take the plunge. Have a lovely big breakdown. Go on! Just do it! Don't hold back. What is a fucking breakdown anyway? What is it really like to have one? There are two exits left open to all of us. One is a breakdown. The other is suicide. That was Jessie's exit. And Valerie's mother's exit. Was there someone else she was forgetting? Had someone else gone out that door? When you have children those exits are closed. Once you have children you are no longer free to do as you like with your life. Does everyone know this before they have children? Or does it come as a surprise? Margie was born during the night. An easy birth. Out she came. Pink and ready to make a go of it. And three days later Tom drove us both home. It took a couple of weeks—or was it months? Then I woke up one morning knowing I had paid with my life for the privilege of motherhood. I stood by her cot looking at her sleeping. An angel in my life. The new owner had moved in. Perfect, fresh, smelling divine, an angel from heaven. From then on, I was renting my space from her. I still am. I can move a little left or right, or I can stay on track, in line, but I'm not the owner anymore. My ownership of my life was finished the night you were born, Marguerite! My life no longer belonged to me, except when I was so far away and in such a deeply foreign place that I really did forget for a blissful moment that I was responsible for you two. In Hefei I became a foreigner in my own life and I was free. I loved it. I fucking loved it! I met the other in me. My private foreigner. Just for one night. Free to betray you all, or to hang myself. An image of Jessie fitting the smooth skein of the dressing-gown cord around her neck, fitting it with care, with love, before she fell into the eternity from which she had come when she emerged from her own mother's womb. Her mother's womb. Just to make some sense of it all. Fran put her hand to her face to deal with an itch. Her fingers came away wet and she realised she was crying. So what? We cry when we need to cry. She felt his weight come onto the settee beside her, the weight of the man sitting down on the seat beside her on the bus as it travelled through the misty rain in Hefei. She felt his hand on her thigh and a shiver ran through her.

Tom said, 'You're overwrought.'

'Oh, is that it? Thanks. I wondered what it was.' She took his hand off her thigh.

'Sorry. You've had a rough day.'

'It's not raining, is it?'

'Clear as a bell out there. We'll have a hard frost in the morning.'

She stretched her shoulders and breathed deeply, then let the air out of her lungs. 'I've abandoned my career.'

'Good. I'm glad to hear it.'

'What will we do for money?'

'I've never worried about money. I'll get a job with one of the builders around here. Carpenters are hard to find. I'll have more work than I can poke a stick at.'

'Splendid.'

He looked at her. 'Seriously.'

'Yes, I know you're being serious. What about your dream?'

'Dreams. Well, that's what they are. Then you wake up. What about your dream of being a professor?'

'I don't want to talk about it. I've fucked up.'

She realised the noise she'd been vaguely aware of for a while was Margie and Tommy playing with Jenny in the passage between their rooms. 'We should let Margie go and live with your mother if she really wants to,' she said. 'I'm just being selfish trying to keep her here. She couldn't do any worse than I've done. Your mum's lovely. I'd trust her with Margie. I just didn't feel comfortable with that boy.'

'Perhaps we should let Margie decide about him.'

'If anything happens to her, I'll feel guilty for the rest of my life.'

'It's about her, not us. We feel guilty anyway. Even if nothing happens to her.'

'There's no way out really, is there?'

'You want to get out?'

'Sometimes.'

'Like right now?'

'Ten minutes ago, I'd have given anything. A bit less now. I'd regret it by the morning. You're fetching Joseph. We'll need to be a bit normal for him. Poor man.'

'That big hearth draws beautifully. The big room must have been a happy place. It warmed up at once. I reckon he'll love it there. I wouldn't mind living there myself. He might have a job getting his dog back from Tommy, that's all. I think those two bonded on sight.'

'Yes, he'll love the cottage. He's a gardener. Maybe he and Ina will hit it off. Sitting up there on her stony ridge with those goats and her garden. If she runs into Joseph, I reckon she'll know a soul mate.'

'You're already matchmaking.'

'Just dreaming.'

They were silent for a long time.

He said, 'I don't know whether I should say this or not.'

'Say it.' She looked at him. 'Just say it.'

'Well, you've abandoned your dream.'

'I've grown out of it.'

'And it looks like I've abandoned mine. What do you think? We've always lived with our dreams till now.'

'We could be in for a long routine.'

'Don't take to drink, will you?'

She held up her glass and smiled. 'Maybe I will. Who knows? This is lovely wine. We won't be able to afford it. If we're no longer dreamers, maybe being drunks will be some compensation.'

He said, 'Tommy's a dreamer.'

'I wonder what he writes? Do you think he writes about us?'

'A story without an end, eh?'

'The end of childhood.' She rested her head on his shoulder. 'Have you really given up?'

'Being a craftsman? Probably not. I love it when I'm in my groove. It's like finding myself each time. And losing everything else. Just for an hour or two.'

'I envy you. I had that feeling. Once.'

'When was that?'

'I'm not telling.'

He was staring at her. He stood up and pulled her up with him. 'You go and hop into bed. You look tired. Really tired.'

'I feel emptied out.'

'What happens now?'

'We just go on, I suppose.'

'It doesn't seem like enough. Just going on.'

'We don't have a choice. We don't belong to ourselves anymore. I dreamed I'd lost you. It was a nightmare. I was alone. When I woke up, I thought at first it was a dream of loss and guilt. But it was just a dream of the truth. Not the domestic make-believe we live by, but the pitiless truth: that we are alone.'

FOUR

Tommy was up in the sunlight, edging his way out towards the topmost limb of the old tree. The central limb of the tree was dead, the bark grey and crumbly. The limb on which Tommy's weight rested was the only remaining part of the tree that was still alive and bearing a few leaves and fruit. The limb branched into several smaller limbs towards its upper end. On a couple of these outer branches there were the small, hard, dark-skinned nectarines, like polished agates in the sunlight. Joseph stood to one side underneath Tommy, looking up at him and holding the bucket, which was already half filled with the small fruit. It was late afternoon. The sun was still hot. Joseph was wearing his old brown trilby, his gardening hat, the sleeves of his grey shirt rolled to his elbows, his forearms browned and sinuous. The summer had been dry. It hadn't rained for months and the flats below the ridge were baked to an even, powdery fawn. Despite the heat, Jenny and Ina's kelpie were chasing each other around the orchard trees. Colours were subdued, as if the long dry summer had faded them, the detail illuminated in the soft golden light of late afternoon. The orchard was old, the trees dead and dying, gaps in the ranks where trees had once thrived, providing Ina and her husband Jim with apples, pears, peaches and nectarines for a whole season of their lives, diminished now, the last of it. The orchard a ruin of time.

The grass and weeds had been eaten to the earth by the goats. Ina's kelpie was brown and white, with black ears. Jenny was as fast as the kelpie, slick on her turns around the orchard trees. They were being watched by three haughty goats lying in the shade of a gum tree beyond the perimeter of the orchard. Tommy was barefoot. Where the soles of his feet gripped the branch, he had broken off small sections of the grey lichen. The lichen appeared to be quite dead and beyond any possibility of recovery, but when the cool weather came, or if there was a late summer storm, it would miraculously come to life again. It was a tree lichen, not the lichen on the brittle rock of the ridge that fascinated Tommy, where the spine of the earth's skeleton broke through the thin topsoil. Joseph was able to see this upthrust spine of stone from where he stood. Along the ridge, at intervals, as if they had been set there with some human intention or design, there were sharp upright slices of triangular rock. Coming on them a stranger might think they had been set there in the past for some ritual purpose. A sign of something that had once had meaning for people—they were so regularly spaced, surely this indicated significance?—but of something we no longer understood.

Ina, who was a familiar of that country, knew the spacing of those stones to lie deeper than mere human intention; she knew it belonged to the period of the creek's source, the springs that rose far beneath the interior of the volcanoes dotting the landscape, ancient beyond human understanding, guardians of the deeper spirit of another existence that did not reckon in human time, but reckoned in the time of stone and fire. Real things, but not human. She knew the country was not hers, but she loved it all the same and was at home in it. Had been born into it. Knew no other place than this. It was where she and Jim had lived their lives together. She was content not to know other places. She was sparing with her opinions and rarely voiced them. The ridge was home. That was it. What else did she need to know? She could not live another life somewhere else and she did not long to do so. She possessed in her poverty all that she needed. Ina Turner, the old woman on the ridge. She was happy. She would die soon, as these trees in the orchard were dying. She was not in pain. She pined for nothing. Jim had gone long ago and still lived in the heart of her vivid memories. It was to him she spoke her private thoughts in the evening and when she worked outside in the trusted company of her dog and the goats. Joseph and Tommy suited her. And after she was dead, Tommy had told her, he would live on the ridge that had given her generously of the years. Ina was not a simple woman, but she was wise enough to know her contentment.

She was sitting on a heavy plank of old timber. The plank was resting on two sawn rounds from the same tree and formed the seat of the bench. She was four or five metres from the base of the nectarine tree and was in the broken shade of a wounded pear tree which had been planted the same year as the nectarine that Tommy was climbing. Ina did not know who had planted the orchard. It was old when she and Jim arrived. When Joseph asked her, she had said, 'The old people planted it.' Whose old people she didn't say. Joseph had been interested to know the age of the trees. Ina was doing something with a basin on her knees. It was not clear to Joseph what she was doing, but whatever it was, it was keeping her fingers busy. She had fashioned the crude bench herself when she was a young woman and her husband was alive and working for the dairy farm that now belonged to the new people, Tom and Frances, Tommy's father and mother. The thick pit-sawn red gum plank of her bench was deeply cratered from weathering and was as grey as the lichen, and as sturdy as on the day she set it there on its two stumpy pillars. There was a steady humming of insects in the air around her and every now and then one of the dogs yelped when the other one became too boisterous. One of the goats stood up and stretched. At a great distance a machine was operating. Perhaps a farmer was baling a late cut of lucerne. It had not been a good year for lucerne, but a few farmers had been able to irrigate small acreages from the creek. The creek below the ridge, which bordered the flats and also marked the western boundary of Frances and Tom's place, had not run dry. Ina had not been surprised by the creek's persistence through the dry summer. She had never seen the springs fail. Earlier, when Joseph and Tommy arrived, she had been splitting firewood, stacking the split wood in the lean-to behind the cottage while it was dry and warm in preparation for the winter to come. If the weather stayed dry, there would be hard frosts. Ina also cooked on a wood stove. She and Jim had not had the cottage put on to the electricity grid when it came through the district. The blocks she had cut with her handsaw were from an old grey box tree which had been ringbarked in the fifties. The blocks were twisted in the grain in such a way it took an expert eye to split them. Ina was not a talker. None of them had learned much about her or her past.

Tommy reached out as far as he could, until his fingers touched the greyish leaves. He edged forward another inch and got his fingers around the twig from which the three shiny nectarines were hanging. Joseph called, 'Careful, Tommy! That will do! Don't go any further. We can knock them down with a rake handle.' But Tommy was determined to get these last nectarines himself. He had set out to do it. He loved knowing that Joseph admired him. It was not that he was unafraid. He had thrilled with a shot of adrenaline when he launched himself onto the topmost branch. The butterflies in his stomach had settled now and he knew he was not going to give up.

'Tommy . . .' Joseph pleaded quietly, watching the boy risking himself. Ina looked up from her task at the concern in Joseph's voice. It was Ina who had seen at once that Tommy was the little boy whom Joseph and his wife had longed for but never had. She had listened in silence to Joseph's story, the pair of them sitting in her kitchen, knowing each other as old people do. Just people together. She smiled to herself now and said, 'Old Joseph has become a grandfather. He didn't expect that, did he?' And she resumed stringing the beans. Although no one had heard her speak, she felt she had spoken to someone. It was just as satisfying as if someone had been there listening to her. In Tommy she had seen a determined, elderly sort of boy, small of stature and slim, with a strangely direct intensity about him, as if he knew his path in life and had no doubt of his ability to fulfil it. She liked him thoroughly. There was nothing of him she didn't like and she was grateful for his friendship. That she didn't really know his mother didn't trouble her. His mother had come up onto the ridge and introduced herself and had sat in the kitchen and drunk her tea, but no contact had really been made between them. Tommy said he would put his desk in the kitchen when he lived there. The single window overlooked the flats and the fields beyond the creek and he said he would write his books there in the morning and after lunch would work on the acreage. 'I shall replant the orchard,' he said, standing at the window looking out. 'Beside each dead tree I will plant a tree of the same kind, as if it is the child of the original tree. And I shall never remove the dead trees.'

'I've got them, Joseph!' Tommy called, the three hard little globes now in his grasp. He looked down at Joseph and smiled, and he extended his hand down as far as he could, until Joseph reached up. 'Drop them!' Joseph said.

Tommy let go of the three nectarines and Joseph caught two of them in his right hand and dropped them into the bucket, then bent down and picked up the other from the grass. 'Well done! Be careful coming down!'

Tommy was inching his way backwards along the living branch.

Ina was no longer watching. Jenny and the kelpie had gone down to the creek to cool off. The two goats that had remained lying down were watching the scene with indifference. Bearded and intelligent, so they seemed, knowing something the humans did not know. Beautiful creatures from another world. Perhaps

Ina knew what the goats knew. Or perhaps she was content to know that she did not know it, incurious herself and untroubled when she neither knew nor understood a thing. After a month or two of living in the cottage, Joseph said to Fran one evening at dinner, 'Ina lives with the mysteries.'

Tommy made it down to safety on the ground. He looked into the bucket. 'Pretty good, eh?'

Joseph looked into the bucket with him. 'Let's give them to Ina. You take them.'

* * *

When Tommy went in the back door later, he heard his father talking on the phone in the living room. He stood and listened. Tom was talking to Margie. Tommy heard him say, 'You'd better stick it out and finish the year, though, darling.' Tommy knew his sister was suffering from homesickness. The home-sickness had taken her by surprise. His father and mother talked about it almost every mealtime. His mother had done a complete flip from her original reluctance to let Margie go and live in England and now wanted to let her come home at once. 'I can't stand the thought of her missing us over there. It breaks my heart.' Tommy knew that his sister's unhappiness at her grandmother's place in Somerset didn't really break his mother's heart and he didn't take the whole thing too seriously. He heard his father say, 'Your mother's not here, darling.' This was followed by a moment of silence, then his father said, 'She's in Melbourne today visiting Valerie. I'll get her to give you a call when she gets home.'

Tommy stopped listening to what his father was saying on the phone and went into the bathroom and peed, then washed his hands and examined his face in the medicine cabinet mirror. 'It's me again,' he said happily to his reflection. When he came out of the bathroom his father was still on the phone. He was, Tommy thought, arguing quietly with Margie, which he didn't think was a good idea. Instead of going to his room and resuming his writing, as he would have done before Joseph and Jenny came to live on the farm, he went out the back door and ran down to the cottage—skipped, actually.

Fran stepped out of the shower. The air was so dry she hardly needed the towel. She put on her green dressing-gown and dried her hair with the hair dryer, then went into the bedroom and opened the mirrored door of the wardrobe. The house was silent and empty around her. She stood looking at herself. So, look at you, Frances Egan, she said. You're nobody now. How does it feel to be no longer Dr Frances Egan, head of the School of Management at the university? Now you're just Fran Egan, the newcomer from the city, the tree changer on the farm under Nortons Ridge. A woman without a history.

She stepped up to the wardrobe and fingered the soft black wool weave of the expensive suit she'd bought less than six months earlier. The suit had given her great pleasure, but it hadn't in the end saved her. You looked good, Fran. Fit and trim, heading out the door in the morning to catch the commuter train, your husband watching you, admiring you. Then you were out there in public, sitting on the train looking out the window, dreaming of your lover. So that was all really just one big lie, was it? Just one elaborately infantile deception? Is that what it was? And if it was that, then what is this now?

She stepped back and stood frowning at the dresses and suits and the smart skirts and tops hanging there. And just look at those lovely shoes! My God, what a waste. Should I feel ashamed? Are you ever going to wear any of this stuff again? Ever? I mean, is it really over? Is this really it? It's not so simple, is it? So, you flew. So what? You took a flying leap from the cliff into the void. The woman who flew. Then what did she do? Is she going to become the woman who crashed to earth and never got back on her feet again? The woman who started drinking that third glass of wine every evening? What will your mother say? So, darling, it was all for nothing after all, was it? That PhD and all those prizes. That's what she'll say. Fran could hear her mother saying it, that know-all look of a fatal world in her mother's eyes, looking off out the window of her house in Ballyragget at the grey sky. 'Thank God I didn't go there in the end.'

She picked up the shorts she'd been wearing for the past few days and pulled them on. Then she put on her bra and slipped the pale green t-shirt with the Nike logo over her head, and she closed the wardrobe door and went out into the kitchen. She was glad she had the place to herself. Tommy was at school and Tom was subcontracting with the builder Rob Shears. He was going like the clappers, he said. His skills as a carpenter and cabinet-maker were in high demand. He was the breadwinner at last. Was it all slipping back into the old standard arrangement then? Could she face the nothingness of that? She stood at the window looking over the paddocks, her yellow Renault's back end catching the sun. Another hot summer day. Not a breath of wind. Just the dry heat. The pastures dead and hard. Joseph had brought up a beautiful bunch of spinach. It was lying on the draining board. Alongside the gloss of the green spinach, he had laid a single perfect rosebud, the deep warm red of Mr Lincoln, the rose with the heady perfume. Fran picked up the rosebud and held it to her nose and she closed her eyes. Joseph was never awkward in his gratitude to her, but always found some gentle way of expressing it. She put the stem in a tumbler of water then stood a long time looking out the kitchen window doing absolutely nothing. The morning was progressing, the shadows of the fence posts already shortening. The weight of that place had lifted from her shoulders. She was free. The big question of what she was actually going to do could wait a while yet. The answer was on its way. Sometimes these things move slowly. They can't be rushed. Rush things and you lose the worth of them. They don't thank you. She would wait. She would learn to work in the garden with Joseph. They might grow a crop of something to sell at the farmers' market.

She picked up their reliable old stove-top percolator and unscrewed it. 'Anyway,' she said aloud to the room, 'there's no way back. That road is closed.'

The percolator was still warm and there was a drop of Tom's morning coffee left in it. She took it to pieces and ran the cold water into it then packed it with fresh coffee, put it on the stove and turned on the gas. The gas pressure was down. They probably needed a new tank. Tom had been looking after these things since they'd come to the farm, while she was busy getting on with the farce of becoming someone important.

She stood watching the percolator, hearing it beginning to murmur, the smell of the coffee starting to fill the kitchen. She had a moment of feeling enormously privileged. It was slightly scary. It was her mother who made it scary. She could hear her saying it, casting her doubts into the mix: So what now, Frances Egan?

It occurred to her that her mother had only ever stepped in and taken the witness stand when things weren't going well. Hadn't she always really been for the prosecution? Her mother had surely found a perverse and fatalistic satisfaction in seeing her daughter fail. Waiting for it, as if failure were a certainty, her fate and doom. Fran's brilliant year twelve results and the successful publication of her PhD had drawn from her mother only the most grudging of acknowledgements. It was her father who had been liberal in his encouragement. Maybe her mother would have been satisfied if she'd seen the whole world fail? So there! I could have told you all. Returning to her home village and the Church after the death of her husband. Reducing her life to its shrouded beginnings. Becoming her own meagre past. Fran suddenly saw her own action in quitting her job as the kind of thing her mother might have done; getting danger-ously close to success, and beginning to fear it. Was that it? Were they terrified of succeeding? As a family, did she and her mother court failure? Did they believe failure was their real fate? Their due?

The smell of the percolating coffee lifted Fran's spirits. Her mother's gloomy predictions wilted and vanished at Fran's antici-pation of standing in the warm sun on the back deck looking out over the flats to the creek, cradling a mug of coffee in her hand. Fran poured the dark aromatic liquid into her favourite owl mug and carried it out the back door. Tom had put in the deck himself. It was the first thing he had done after they bought the farm. Standing out there in the summer morning she was at once calmer, the familiar smell of the eucalypts drawn from the leaves by the heat. Joseph was down there in the garden he had made beside the cottage, his dark form crouched among his plants. Tom was pretty good at growing vegetables, but Joseph was in another class altogether. Somehow, he had grown flowers and vegetables through the dry summer, harvesting the limited water of the cottage. Jenny was a little white blob curled up asleep in the deep shade of the kurrajong tree. The tree must have been planted when the stone cottage was built. It wasn't local. It reassured her to see Joseph and Jenny down there. She felt good knowing they were safe from the managers at the university. She drank the hot coffee. Whether it was her mother or herself who asked the question, it did actually have to be asked: What now, Fran? It was sure to be the biggest question for which life was going to demand an answer from her now. And how she answered it would surely determine the rest of her life. She knew that. She needed this time alone to think. The worst of it was when she was lying sleepless beside Tom at night and at her most vulnerable; that was when the panic shrieked at her to crawl back into the trap from which she had liberated herself. *You can still become a professor!* it yelled. *Fucking do it! What happened to you?* In the night that voice made her sweat with fear. When daylight came it lost its power and she wondered why the night made her such a victim to it. And when she was with Valerie, the voice in her head changed its tune completely. Belief returned. *You have liberated yourself from an illusion.*

She did have an idea. It was not yet firmly established. But it was an idea and she held on to it. It was all she had. She nurtured it. She had touched on it the last time she was with Valerie. They were sitting at the table in Valerie's cluttered kitchen and Valerie was showing her the collection of notebooks. It was her account of her life, all of it addressed to Jessie, the years in London with Phillipa, the travel on the Continent, Tunisia, and her own interior beliefs and thoughts, the poetry and the intimate reflections, the periods of despair and the periods of hope. Valerie's world, a beautiful, pained world of reflection and love, of suffering and torture, and the madness of the voices. Joseph understood.

'I began to write after Jessie's suicide. Much of it of course happened long before I met Jessie. It is my supplementary reality. Without writing I would have killed myself long ago. Writing saved me.'

'You mean you weren't actually in Sidi Bou Said when you wrote about it?'

Valerie looked thoughtful and shook her head, her thin grey hair drifting across her face. 'I couldn't have written about it while I was there experiencing it. I was too close to it to see it. I began to write after I became a patient in the nut house. It was then that I discovered that facts are not the only truth. Our own private truth is elusive and hides from us. It is the truth the poets seek. Remembering at night alone in that cell saved me, and I began to live a life of the memory. I learned to cultivate my memory, to attend to it with love, the way Joseph and Mr Cool cultivated the gardens they tended. I was glad to be alone and locked in. I knew no one would come to disturb me. The more deeply I entered into my memories the more memory opened to me. Memories I had not known I possessed. Secret, dark places in which small clues had lain buried for years. Searching the landscapes of memory became for me a journey of discovery. Before I understood that I could open the secret doors of memory, if someone had asked me to tell them about my childhood, I would have said I had few memories of it. It takes time and love for the garden of memory to compose its stories. Real life was unbearable for me. It was unbearable for all of us in that place. Many didn't survive. Many who had been troubled but really quite sane when they arrived there went mad. Isn't it what we humans have always done? What are the fairy stories of our childhood? They are where we live happily ever after. They are memorials to the deeper truth we yearn for, the truth that sustains us and gives us a reason to persist. I still do it. Every evening alone in my dead father's old house, this great cold house where my mother killed herself rather than have another child, I write in my journals. I open the door to memory and leave the awfulness behind. In my journals, as in my dreams, I am still young.'

She got down on the floor, sighing and groaning, and brought all the notebooks out from the cupboard beside the sink, handing them up to Fran like some old peasant unearthing potatoes. Fran took them from her and set them down on the table. Many of them had taken on the musty smell of the house, their covers curled and stained, and when Valerie lifted them off the boards silverfish scattered.

'Everything I've written is to Jessie. She has always been my inspiration.' With her head in the cupboard her voice was muffled and she coughed. 'I have written about what I have most loved. I have told her everything. I have shared every good and intimate thing with Jessie. She has remained my life's companion.' She handed up the last of them and Fran helped her to get up onto her feet. 'While I am writing I am no longer this scraggy helpless old bag. With my pen in my hand at night I am transformed into the fairy queen. My pen is my magic wand. I have shared my life with Jessie.' She placed a hand on the nearest pile, as if she meant to swear an oath on the Bible. 'It is all here. This is our world. Jessie's and mine. Our real world. The life of our dreams. It is all written with love.' She paused, looking at her wrinkly old hand covering the notebooks. Then she looked up at Fran. 'I've never shown these to anyone, Fran. No one has ever read any of it till Joseph gave you the one I lost. I have never thought of anyone reading it. It was written for her and for myself.'

Fran was moved and she embraced Valerie. Valerie laughed with delight and put her arms around Fran. 'You're such a darling.'

They sat side by side at the table. Valerie lit a cigarette and sat looking at the collection on the table. 'I have never read it. I wrote it. But I've never read it. When I fill a notebook I set it aside and turn to the new one. I have never been back to read over what I've written. Reading the notebook you returned to me was the first time I read myself. I was moved. We can't go back in life and repeat something or change it once it's done. I wasn't writing to make it sound good. I was talking to Jessie.' She drew on her cigarette and studied Fran for some time. 'I've never thought before this of ever having a reader. I've never thought about it. I write every day. When I came home to take care of Dad during his final years, I began putting the notebooks in that cupboard. Jessie was never in this house. Now I think the diary Joseph rescued was special. I think it was unique. He gave you the key to the whole story. The key to my survival in that place. When you gave the book back to me that day, you brought it all into my mind again in a great rush, in a way I'd never seen it before. And when you began to tell me later on how much that little book meant to you, it was only then that I too began to see that my writing might be read, might have readers, might mean something to women like you and me and not just to Jessie.'

She fell silent, smoking her cigarette, her eyes narrowed, studying Fran. 'You told me what I had done, Fran. I didn't know what I had done until you responded so richly to it and let me see it through your eyes. I began to see that my life might not have been a wasteland after all.'

Fran said, 'Your life and your writings and your friendship, they are an inspiration to me. There is a great book in them. It should be shared.'

Valerie said, 'The title of that book would be *Jessie's World*. We do share it, you and I. You've made me see it. You've made it worthwhile to me in a way it could not have been before you came into my life. I often thought of throwing out all these notebooks with the recycling. Not the little diary you brought me. Not that one. I didn't have that one. I thought someone had stolen it. Friendship is not one way, my dear. You also have given me hope. Until you responded to my work with your own sense of wonder, I had written without anyone in mind apart from Jessie. It is with her I have shared the story. The one person who gave me confidence and who I knew would grant me her understanding no matter how clumsy my expression. With her I have felt at liberty to write as I speak inside my own head, with my own secret voice.'

'I would love to try putting it all together. Your story. Your words. The two of you. Your lives. It's such a beautiful story.'

Valerie ashed her cigarette in her cup. 'Well, why not? Let's do it.' She reached across the table and picked up the original notebook that Joseph had rescued and she handed it to Fran. 'This is yours. It's where we began.'

Fran said, 'I couldn't possibly take it from you.'

'What bloody nonsense! Take it! Its life is with you now. You are my reader. I know you love it. It's you who has given all this a life.' She put her hand on Fran's hand. 'I'm happy to be alive since I met you. I was ready to leave when you turned up.'

Fran couldn't speak for the emotion in her breast.

Valerie laughed. 'Just look at you! You're such a softie.'

'I'm sorry.'

'Take it!' Valerie held the diary out. 'You're young. Take it.'

Fran reached and took the little book in her hand.

Valerie said, 'I'll think of you reading it while you are sitting by that sacred creek of yours with its mystical springs. The innocence of your hopes has survived that madhouse. The poet in you may yet find her voice through my work and begin to speak. What do you think?'

'Oh, Valerie! What you say gives me some hope.'

'Well, it's nothing to be ashamed of, is it. Poetry never did anyone any harm, except to the poets themselves, poor devils.' She paused, then she closed her eyes and quoted from her poem: *'Jessie is my warrior. / I worship her. / I write my love poetry to her with my eyes. / In their sunlit depths antique visions / Of a buried world are preserved, / For her alone.*' She opened her eyes and regarded Fran. 'You have your noble warrior and I have mine. We're not so different, Fran. Our lives are our secrets. And now we'll make this book together.' She paused. 'You can come here and we can work on it together, if you can stand this place. Though I suppose you have a lovely room in your home where you like to work.'

Fran said, 'Let me have a think. I'll come back and see you in a couple of days and we can do some planning.'

They stood up and embraced.

Valerie said, 'I smell awful. Old people smell of their decay.'

'You smell lovely.'

'Life, Frances, it's such a brief affair.' They stood away from each other, Valerie holding on to Fran's hand. 'You'd better get going or you'll find yourself stuck in the heavy traffic and that husband of yours will have burned the dinner waiting for you.'

'I wish you could come out to the farm with me and see the creek.'

'I see it already. I see it with you. You have admitted me to its beauty and its mystery.' She shook another cigarette from the packet and lit it. 'Now be off with you! I need my nap. You've exhausted me.' She laughed and coughed and gestured for Fran to leave. 'Memory is a deep well. Our treasure is down there if we reach for it. The stories in our memory are a story of love. Drive carefully, my dear. And come back and see me again in a couple of days. We'll talk some more about what we will do with all this. I'm curious now. You have seen something in my words that I didn't know was there.' She laughed. 'You are my reader! I need you. Jessie will love you too. Don't worry. I've never envied the sane people of this world.'

When Fran walked down to the cottage that afternoon to ask Joseph to join the family for the evening meal, the door was open. She called, but there was no answer from him. She went in. Despite the oppressive heat of the day, the air in the big room was a pleasant temperature. The thick stone walls retained the cool of the nights and gave out their coolness during the hot summer days. She saw that Joseph had placed the green parrot on the timber mantel above the wide hearth. The woman in the Hefei market from whom she had purchased the parrot had been right. The parrot sat alone on the left of the mantel, where Joseph had put it. It looked to its right, as if Joseph had understood that it was waiting for its mate. But there was no mate for it. The rest of the mantelpiece was empty. Fran went over and touched the parrot. She ran the pads of her fingers lightly over its rounded shape, her eyes half closed, running her fingers over the silky skin of his thighs. A sound behind her made her snatch her hand away guiltily. Joseph was in the doorway with his back to her. He had one hand to the frame and was leaning down removing his boots. Fran watched him. Jenny came in and ran up to Fran and leaped at her. Fran bent down to her. The vast secret longing for her lover would return to claim her, she knew that, and knowing it made her happy.

Joseph turned around and came into the room.

She said, 'Thank you for the rose and the spinach. Come up and have a meal with us later. I'm roasting a leg of lamb on the barbecue.'

Joseph did not respond at once but stood looking at her. He saw the uncertainty in her smile and said, 'You can't know how much it means to me, dear Fran, to be here with you and Tom and your Tommy.'

* * *

She was standing at the kitchen sink peeling potatoes. The lamb was cooking slowly on the barbecue out on the front deck. She watched the truck turn in from the road, dust billowing behind it. Tom was driving fast. She could see Tommy sitting up next to him. When Tom walked in he said, 'God, I'm bloody famished. That meat smells fantastic.' He came over to her and kissed her cheek.

'You smell of beer,' she said.

He was flushed and full of confidence. He kissed her firmly on the lips then stepped away. 'And you smell of love.'

She laughed.

'Rob and I stopped off at the Newstead pub and had a couple of jars. And guess what? I've had two new orders for specials. Rob's customers tell him they love that red gum island bench I made for the new couple out at Yapeen. Rob says I could double what I'm asking for those handmade pieces. He's probably right.'

'That's wonderful!'

'I'm going to have a quick shower. And Tommy got an A for his maths test, by the way.'

'Where is Tommy?'

'I think he went straight down to tell his new mate. For the first time in his life, our little Tommy has two friends.'

She finished the potatoes and put them in the oven. Tom was singing in the shower. She poured a glass of wine and took it out onto the front deck. The air was noisy with birds. What startling news had the birds received? Crows and white cockatoos and a whole gang of corellas and the magpie family. The rooster joining in, sitting on the top bar of the gate. The poor flightless rooster. The others were all diving and calling and challenging each other, showing off their magical skills, empowering the air with flight. The sun was going down more slowly than usual, lingering on the horizon, the shadow of the big red gum edging across the paddock. A faint remnant of Tom's dust lingering there. She drank from her glass. The flocks of birds entered the cover of the tree's canopy and fell silent, unseen now, the air empty, as if they had all received the same signal, the command. Enough! Enough.

The following Tuesday afternoon great black and green and white thunderheads bloomed higher and higher into the stratosphere in the eastern sky. A show of force was being prepared. Already the distant rumbling of the approaching storm. Fran was naked, floating on her back in the pool at the creek, her body cooled by the magical spring water. Her clothes and a towel lay in a bundle on the bank. The light was powerful, dramatic, gold and brassy, a light show before the storm, the air glowing with the day's heat, the dry earth holding its breath, waiting for the rain. The birds were silent, hidden among the foliage of the trees. Fran could sense their apprehension.

A pair of galahs flew across above her, calling to each other, racing the storm . . . and she remembered Sanjeev's visit to her when she was packing to leave her room at the university. He came to the door of her office behind her and she turned from packing books into a carton. He said, 'I came to say goodbye and to wish you well for your future.' She was deeply touched. 'I'll miss you, Sanjeev.' She dropped the book she was holding into the carton. 'I'm giving them to the library.' She turned to him. 'I don't really know what I'm doing. One moment I'm sure I've liberated myself from a trap, and the next I feel as if I've lost my way.'

Sanjeev smiled and said with quiet conviction, 'You will find your way.' His words moved her, they had stayed with her. She believed him.

She stepped out of the creek and stood on the bank. The water glistened on her skin, the light of the last of the day gilding her nakedness. The mysterious depths from which the springs had their origins. She stood absorbing the light, knowing her beauty confidently at that moment, thinking of her lover, dwelling in her imagination with her noble Mongol warrior. She said, 'I am a goddess for you.' She smiled then bent and picked up the towel and dried herself off. She had called Margie earlier and told her their home news. It was like speaking to a friend. Margie was changing. Then, at the end of the call,

Margie had cried to think of her family missing her, and she was a little girl again.

Fran pulled on her shorts and her t-shirt. The thunder was louder, lightning stabbing into the horizon. Storm clouds had already obliterated the western slopes. It was roaring over there, thrashing through the timber, howling and releasing its deluge. Fran said aloud: 'Without love, imagination is dead.' It felt like an important insight for her. Having such a thought come into her mind made her feel young. As if she might live forever.

Walking across the grassy flat towards the hill and her home, the earth warm against the soles of her feet, she was eager to begin reading the hoard of Valerie's notebooks. She had waited, she had been patient, and her new purpose had been given to her by her friend. The first touch of rain fell on her bare arm as she spoke aloud Valerie's poem to her lover: *'Am I not her love? / Her valiant saluki? / Her hound of heaven? / My gaze that of a poet dreaming / Of hunting with my mistress.'* Fran heard her own consolation, her sense of possibility and new purpose in Valerie's lines. The promise of her own new beginning. Valerie's trust, her friendship and her hoard of notebooks offered her something so much greater than the humdrum of the daily make-believe. She had left that illusion behind her for good and would never be tempted to return to it.

There was so much to be done. She would write Valerie's life. She would edit Valerie's papers. She would find a publisher for them. *Jessie's World* would be a jointly authored work of love. She would enter the mysterious beauty of that world of suffering and hope and imagination. Valerie had been astonished when she told her she had visited Sidi Bou Said with Tommy. 'Could that brief account of mine really have meant so much to you that you actually went there?' Fran told her, 'You gave it a life that I longed to be a part of.' Valerie's amazement that her writing might move another person in such a way. Her deep pleasure that in Fran she had discovered the first reader of her work and had sensed the power for others of her own private meandering, what she had called her supplementary reality. Perhaps it could give that enrichment to others too.

The rain was coming down hard. Fran stood and lifted her face to the downpour, her eyes closed. She was soaked in a moment. She was laughing. After all, she was young and beautiful and filled with wonder and hope for the journey that had opened before her.

ACKNOWLEDGEMENTS

I wish to acknowledge the work of my brilliant publisher and friend of more than twenty years and fifteen books, Annette Barlow. Thank you, Annette! Your loyalty and deep concern for my work over the years have meant more to me than I can easily express. I am a fortunate writer indeed to have had the support of your literary intelligence over the years. My work has greatly benefited from the quiet persistence of your guidance, your gentle nudges in the right direction whenever a nudge was needed—which has been often—and your generous enthusiasm at all times. Without your insight and care, and the ever-professional support of your team, my books would be much reduced in quality.

My wife, Stephanie, remains my most astute critic. Since writing my very first book, I have depended on Stephanie's critical readings of my manuscripts. She has rescued me more times than I care to remember from despair and from being utterly lost in my helpless search for the simplicity of a story's structure. Without Stephanie's support I would have completed nothing of worth.

I would also like to express my gratitude for the fine work on the manuscript of this book of my editors, Ali Lavau, Tom Bailey-Smith and Clara Finlay.

ALEX MILLER is the award-winning author of thirteen books and a collection of essays and stories. His work is published internationally and widely in translation. Miller is twice winner of the Miles Franklin Literary Award, in 1993 for *The Ancestor Game* and in 2003 for *Journey to the Stone Country*. He is an overall winner of the Commonwealth Writers' Prize in 1993 for *The Ancestor Game*. *Conditions of Faith* and *Lovesong* are both winners of the Christina Stead Prize for Fiction in the NSW Premier's Literary Awards. In 2012, *Autumn Laing* received the Melbourne Prize for Literature for its outstanding contribution to Australian cultural life. *Coal Creek* won the Victorian Premier's Literary Award in 2014. Alex's twelfth novel, *The Passage of Love*, published in 2017, is his most autobiographical work, a deeply moving masterpiece of the writer's early struggles and loves from the vantage of old age. *Max* was Alex's first work of non-fiction and was shortlisted for the National Biography Award in 2021.